ALETA
AND THE QUEEN

ALETA
AND THE QUEEN

A TALE OF ANCIENT GREECE

Written by Priscilla Galloway
Illustrated by Normand Cousineau

Annick Press Ltd.
Toronto • New York

© 1995 Priscilla Galloway (text)
© 1995 Normand Cousineau (art)
Designed by Primeau Dupras

Annick Press Ltd.

Annick Press gratefully acknowledges the support of the Canada Council
and the Ontario Arts Council.

Canadian Cataloguing in Publication Data
Galloway, Priscilla, 1930-
Aleta and the queen: a tale of ancient Greece

(Tales of ancient lands)
ISBN 1-55037-400-1

I. Cousineau, Normand. II. Title. III. Series:
Galloway, Priscilla, 1930- . Tales of ancient lands.

PS8563.A45A84 1995 jC813'.54 C95-930867-9 PZ7.G35Al 1995

The art in this book was rendered in ink and gouache.
The text was typeset in Perpetua and Lithos.

Distributed in Canada by: Firefly Books Ltd.
250 Sparks Avenue, Willowdale, ON M2H 2S4

Published in the U.S.A. by Annick Press (U.S.) Ltd.
Distributed in the U.S.A. by:
Firefly Books (U.S.) Inc.
P.O. Box 1338, Ellicott Station, Buffalo, NY 14205

Printed and bound in Canada by Metropole Litho, Montréal

CONTENTS

ACKNOWLEDGEMENTS

Many people, alive and dead, have helped in the creation of this tale. Mythographer R.M.H. Shepherd, Professor Emeritus of Classical Studies, University of Toronto, provided expert advice about ancient literary sources, lent me translations and flagged relevant information. British archaeologist Richard Hubbard provided a wealth of detail about the flora and fauna of bronze-age Ithaca and about the people's lives. Research in the Robarts Library, University of Toronto, and in the incomparable British Library in London, England, has aided authenticity. As well as gathering information, I have become aware of many areas where knowledge is lacking and where I've had to make an informed guess. Sources, ancient and modern, often provide alternative or conflicting information. The relationship between Penelope and Clytemnestra, for instance, is not found in Homer. Apollodorus, a later writer, says Penelope's father Icarius was brother to Tyndareus, father of Clytemnestra. This is a story, not a scholarly treatise, however; I've used what seems useful.

My love affair with *The Odyssey* began when I was eight years old. Two translations have been constant companions during my writing of *Aleta and the Queen*, a scholarly version by E.V. Rieu, and a poetic one by Robert Fitzgerald. I am grateful to both, though far more so to Homer, the far-off genius who wrote the two greatest epic poems of our civilization.

Rick Wilks of Annick Press has ably trodden the editor's hard road. His enthusiasm for this book and for the series is an ongoing inspiration. My husband, Howard Collum, has been a constant source of loving support.

PROLOGUE

In Homer's wonderful old story poem, *The Odyssey*, Queen Penelope stayed at home on the rocky island of Ithaca while her husband King Odysseus went off to fight at Troy. Homer's story, however, isn't about Penelope as much as it is about her husband and her son. My story of Aleta began with Penelope and the people at her court and some of the gods and goddesses they believed in. Gods and goddesses in the old stories often disguised themselves as people, but they had special powers. Some of them were friends to the people in this story, while others were enemies.

This story took place more than three thousand years ago. King Odysseus and the other warriors fought with bronze swords and shields, though many people still used flint knives, especially in the country. Homer created his poems about Troy and Odysseus (the *Iliad* and *The Odyssey*) approximately four hundred years later. In his time, stories of Troy belonged to a heroic past that never exactly existed, like our stories of King Arthur or Robin Hood. Many of Homer's details belong to the time when he lived, some to the time when the story took place, and some he made up. Like fiction writers and poets everywhere, Homer told his tale the way he thought it should be.

I made up the story of Aleta and her mother, using people and events in the *Odyssey* as a starting place, including the hundred suitors who moved into the palace and refused to leave until Penelope married one of them. I did research to find out about Ithaca three thousand years ago. We know more today about how those people lived than Homer did. For example, a botanist who studies plant life in ancient times was able to tell me what plants grew wild on the rocky hills of Ithaca, and what others Aleta and her grandmother would have found along the banks of a stream. This does not mean that my story is a substitute for Homer. There is no substitute for Homer. I hope that readers who enjoy my Greek tales will go on later to read his.

The people of ancient Greece lived differently from us, and different things were important to them. Much of their world was mysterious, and they had no scientific way of solving their mysteries. Their society was not technological like ours. They thought the earth was flat. Why then did the sun pass over it each day? What would happen if a ship sailed too near the edge? Who held the stars in place? Stories of gods and heroes solved these mysteries. The fiery chariot of the sun was guided by the god Apollo. Poseidon ruled the seas. Zeus, king of the gods, governed gods and mortals, with his wife Hera at his side and Hermes of the winged sandals as his messenger. Athene, goddess of wisdom and of weaving, had leaped, fully armed, from the forehead of her father Zeus, and a mighty headache she gave him in the process. Through stories like these, the Greeks made sense of their world.

The story of *Aleta and the Queen* takes place on the small island of Ithaca, far away from the greatest cities of Greece. Even by the standards of the time, the people of Ithaca did not live in luxury. The king's palace would have been the biggest residence on the island, but it probably did not have a special room corresponding to our kitchen. Much preparation and cooking of food was done outside, in the courtyard. Homes of ordinary people certainly did not have bathrooms, and nothing in the old stories suggests that Odysseus's palace did either. Some kings and nobles in the mainland cities had bathtubs, however, which would have been located inside their palaces. The high king who led the Greeks in battle against Troy was murdered in his bath.

Greek forces destroyed the great city of Troy in 1193 B.C. after ten years of fighting. At much the same time, in another part of the world, Moses was leading the Israelites in their flight out of Egypt. As the story of *Aleta and the Queen* begins, nine years after the fall of Troy, the fate of the hero Odysseus, Penelope's husband, is still unknown. He has not come home from the war, and nobody knows what has happened to him. Queen Penelope has ruled alone for nineteen years.

PRONUNCIATION OF GREEK NAMES

Greek names are not as difficult as they look. Sound the letters the way you do in English, except as follows:

RULE	EXAMPLE	SOUND
c is usually pronounced as k	Cyclops	Sy'-klops
the final e is not silent	Penelope	Pen-el'-o-pee

"Aleta," "Kleea," "Nesta," "Castor," "Helen" and "Mentor" sound just the way they would in English.

MT. OLYMPUS

TROY

AEGEAN SEA

GREECE

CALYDON

DELPHI

ITHACA

ASIA MINOR

ATHENS

MYCENAE

LACONIA

SPARTA

MEDITERRANEAN SEA

TO CYCLOPS

CRETE

WHO'S WHO:
CHARACTERS IN ORDER OF APPEARANCE

KLEEA (Klee'-ah, short for Eurycleia, Yoo-ree-klee'-ah):
Queen Penelope's housekeeper and trusted companion; nanny to Telemachus and, before him, to his father Odysseus

ALETA (A-lee'-tah):
granddaughter of Kleea, daughter of Nesta

PENELOPE (Pen-el'-o-pee):
Queen of Ithaca, wife of Odysseus

ODYSSEUS (O-diss'-youss or O-diss'-ee-us):
Penelope's husband, King of Ithaca, who went away to war when his son was a baby

TELEMACHUS (Tel-em'-ah-kus):
son of Penelope and Odysseus

NESTA (Ness'-tah):
daughter of Kleea, mother of Aleta, friendly to Penelope's enemies

ATHENE (A-thee'-nee):
goddess of wisdom and of weaving, friendly to Penelope and her family

PHEMIUS (Fee'-mee-us):
singer at the palace

LAERTES (Lay-er'-teez):
father of Odysseus, has retired to his farm

MENTOR (Men'-tor):
advisor to Penelope, teacher of Telemachus

HELEN:
serving woman, friend of Nesta, hostile to Odysseus and his family

ANTINOUS (An-tin'-oh-us)
EURYMACHUS (Yoo-rim'-a-kus or Yoo-ree-ma'-kus)
CASTOR (Kas'-tor):
suitors of Queen Penelope, three of one hundred men who want to marry her

POSEIDON (Po-sy'-don):
god of the sea, enemy to Odysseus

CYCLOPS (Sy'-klops):
one-eyed giant, a monster, son of the sea-god Poseidon

CHAPTER ONE

WILL THE KING
EVER COME HOME?

"Tell me the truth, Grandmother. Will the king ever come home?"

Kleea straightened her back and looked down at the girl. The fleece she had been beating lay on her thigh. The wiry old woman sat on a four-legged stool, the pile of fleeces to be carded at her side. Aleta, who had been sorting them, knelt on the hard-packed mud that paved the courtyard, facing the gate. The morning sun warmed her slim, bare arms. Beyond the gate, the road vanished in heavy woods, but Aleta knew where it led: one way went toward the old king's farm, where Aleta had been born; the other led to the town and the harbour, where long ago King Odysseus had boarded his ship and sailed away to war.

"Why not?" said Kleea. "Haven't I always told you he would come?" Anger rose in her, reddening her face. "You have been listening to those liars in the palace, haven't you."

"Yes," murmured Aleta. She had in fact been listening to her mother, Nesta. She felt ashamed. "I knew you'd know, Grandmother. About the king."

"I do not know." Kleea spoke sharply. "No god has given me a vision, for all my asking. But I've always believed he will come back. His wife and son would draw him home from the gates of death. I don't believe he is dead. After we won the war at Troy, he started home with twelve good ships. Messengers came here, all this way, to bring the news. Perhaps he turned aside to look for riches on his way, and found more than he bargained for. Something must have happened, but not death, surely." Kleea tried to sound totally confident, as usual.

"I remember those messengers. It must have been nine years ago. I wasn't even three years old," Aleta fretted.

Kleea gave up pretending. "The gods alone know what's happened to him. We'll be ruined, and he will have no kingdom to come home to, if he doesn't come home soon." Her faded grey eyes blinked tremulously. Aleta looked shocked, and no wonder. The old woman massaged her hands, willing herself to be calm. What had possessed her to speak like this to the child? Carding wool was good for her bent fingers, the oil soothed and softened her papery skin. Kleea gathered strength around her like a cloak. She picked up another fleece. "Don't you worry, child," she said, in her best grandmother's voice. "Athene has always loved our king. Surely the goddess has him in her hand."

Aleta looked anxiously at the much-loved face. Grandmother looked so much older, suddenly. Aleta bit her tongue. Why had she asked if the king would ever come back?

"Tell me about when the king went away, Grandmother," she coaxed. "You were there, weren't you, holding Prince Telemachus. He was just a baby then."

Kleea smiled. "You are changing the subject, Aleta," she said drily. "You could tell that story as well as I can, you've heard it so often."

"Tell me again."

The fleece dropped from Kleea's hands. Her mind turned back to that long-ago scene. "It was here in the palace, in the queen's own chamber," her storyteller's low voice began. "Little Telemachus was asleep in my arms. He was only a year old, but he was big for his age. My arms were aching. I was his nurse, just like I'd been his father's nurse when *he* was young."

"Mother was there too, wasn't she," said Aleta loyally.

Kleea stiffened. "She had slipped in behind me, but I hadn't noticed. Nesta was always getting in the way."

Aleta swallowed painfully. Ever since she had come to the palace, it seemed, she had been trying not to make the same mistakes as her mother. Time and again she'd stayed out of her grandmother's sight so as not to get in the way. Had she changed the subject again, without wanting to? She did not want Kleea to start in on her mother's faults. "Penelope didn't want the king to go away," she murmured.

Kleea relaxed again. "I remember every word." She did. Even the way the old woman moved took on an echo of the speaker, the dignified young queen. " 'Don't go to war, Odysseus. It's not right. Everybody needs you here.' She was brave, my lady, but her lips were trembling.

"The king turned red. 'By all the gods, Penelope, I have no choice, and well you know it.' That's what he said. 'I swore a sacred oath.' "

"Couldn't he say 'No'?" asked Aleta. "He had a kingdom to rule, and a baby son. He could have told them why he could not keep his oath."

"Aleta! Break a sacred oath! Have I taught you so badly? Better to lose your life than break an oath."

Aleta nodded dutifully. Would she ever understand why a promise was more important than a baby or a wife or a kingdom?

Kleea's shock passed quickly. She went on with her story. "My poor lady was so white! I could see he wanted to wrap his arms around her. His heart was twisted with love. I knew what he was thinking, but of course he would never break his oath." Her grandmother's words twisted in Aleta's heart. " 'It's not as if I *wanted* to leave you,' he told Penelope. 'Remember how I tried to get out of it! Nobody else would have dared.'

" 'I won't forget,' Penelope said. 'You took a chance with our baby's life.'

" 'I never meant to!' the king exclaimed. 'It was a good act, wasn't it. Everybody thought I'd gone crazy.' He was no taller than the queen, but he had grand broad shoulders, and the strongest arms in Ithaca. He was laughing. My lady was looking better, not so white and pinched.

" 'I thought you were mad myself when I saw you dumping salt on the fields.' Penelope shook her head. 'When you yoked up the mule beside the ox and started plowing, I was sure of it. In front of the messenger from Greece!' "

The plowing scene was still sharp in Kleea's mind, as funny as it had been when she had watched it almost twenty years before: the mule, small and fast, and the ox, big and slow, both trying to go different ways at different speeds, and the king dancing along behind them with his plow. She and Aleta laughed together.

" 'I made a fool of myself for nothing,' Odysseus snorted. He looked at his wife, and they both laughed until tears ran down their cheeks.

" 'You should have got away with the trick,' Penelope said at last."

"What trick?" Aleta prompted.

"Pretending he was mad, so the Greeks would release him from his vow," Kleea continued. "There was no other way. Odysseus didn't have a big army, but he was the cleverest fighter, they all knew they could never capture Troy without him. Odysseus would have fooled most people, but the messenger knew him and thought up a trick of his own. He put Telemachus in the field in front of his father's team. 'If the king can't tell the difference between salt and seed, he can't tell the difference between a baby and a clump of dirt,' he said. It was a test."

"The only way for the king to pass that test was to kill his own son." Aleta shuddered.

"That's right," Kleea nodded. "If I had been minding Telemachus that day, they wouldn't have got hold of him, not without killing me first.

" 'It was much too close,' the king said. 'I could see something white on the ground ahead, but I was too busy to wonder what it might be. The mule was pulling one way and the ox the other. It was all I could do to hang onto the plow. Then suddenly I knew that white bundle was Telemachus. I could see his arm. I didn't know if an ox hoof would crush his skull or a mule hoof would brain him. If the hooves missed, the plow could still cut him in half. I will never forget it.'

" 'The gods gave you strength,' Penelope reminded him.

" 'They did,' Odysseus agreed. 'Athene guided me, and I pulled right. It was a tight turn, the plow nearly went over. It missed the baby by this much.' The king held up his hand," said Kleea, "with thumb and little finger outstretched." Aleta shuddered.

" 'Don't complain about my going off to war, dear wife,' the king said at last.

"The queen's hand stroked his cheek. 'It's the price of our son's life, isn't it,' she agreed. 'The gods allowed you to save him. You have no choice. We can both hate it all we like, but the gods demand that you keep your vow. You must take our best men to fight against Troy.'

" 'We could be lucky,' the king told her. 'The Trojans started the fight when they kept Queen Helen. They might do the right thing and give her back. Especially when they see all the kings of Greece ready to batter down their walls. Who knows? I may be home in less than a year.'

" 'Meanwhile, I'll have to do my job and yours too.' The queen's shoulders stiffened. 'It won't be easy for a woman to rule in Ithaca.' Well, I could have told her that!" Kleea exclaimed. "It goes against all custom. Odysseus knew it too.

" 'Let me leave half the soldiers here, under your command,' he suggested."

"Penelope said no," chimed in Aleta. "She told him, 'You need every man. We'll manage, won't we, Kleea.' "

"Her voice trembled a little, but Odysseus didn't notice. I boasted, 'I can use a knife as well as any man,' " sighed Kleea. "I wish either one of us could have seen into the future."

"Then the girl behind you said, 'I'll fight too,' and it was my mother," Aleta burst out.

"Nesta had no sense," snapped Kleea. "I nearly dropped the baby, I was so startled. 'Idiot!' I scolded. 'Get out of here. Go sweep the hall.' "

"You were hard on her." Aleta sighed. Kleea said it herself from time to time. Now she agreed.

"I was hard on her."

"She was little."

"She was as old as you are, nearly." Kleea was disgusted. "Telemachus started howling, and it was all her fault. 'There, there, my darling,' I murmured. I could feel my face getting hot. My daughter had interrupted the king and queen!"

"But they didn't notice," soothed Aleta.

"They might have." Kleea's voice was grim. "But they didn't. Penelope was still talking about soldiers.

" 'The young men want their chance of glory,' she reminded Odysseus. 'There's no war in Ithaca, and not likely to be. Besides, who's to tell if your men would obey me? Are you sure they would let themselves be ruled by a woman?' A good question, wasn't it. It's not for nothing they call her the wise Penelope."

"What did the king say?" Aleta's voice was dreamy.

"He wasn't sure that his men would obey her, I could see that, and he was furious because he wasn't sure. 'Would you rather I left my father in charge?' he asked at last.

"'Don't be ridiculous,' Penelope retorted. 'Your father hasn't ruled this country for years. I love him dearly, but these days he can't keep two ideas in his head, unless it's something to do with his grape vines or his apple trees.'

"'You're right, Penelope,' the king agreed. 'Besides, I may be away for a long time. My father may die before I get home.'

"'You may die yourself,' my brave lady told him quietly. 'War and death go hand in hand. Perhaps you will never come home.'"

Aleta always cried in this part of the story. Without thinking, she wiped her eyes with her grubby hands, redolent with the pungent lanolin smell of the raw wool.

"Odysseus held his finger against his wife's wet cheeks," murmured Kleea, "then against his own lips. 'I will not forget the taste of your tears, Penelope,' he told her. 'I hope to get home, sooner or later, but it may not be that way. If I have not returned by the time Telemachus is grown, then you must find a new husband.' He could hardly get the words out." Kleea's voice faded. "I was crying. Little Telemachus cried so hard he got the hiccups.

"Odysseus took him. His finger must have been rough on the little face, but Telemachus calmed down. He grabbed a handful of his dad's brown curls. They made faces at each other. 'I don't want to leave you,' Odysseus told him, fierce words. He put the precious child into my arms. 'Guard him with your life, Kleea,' he told me."

"And you do, and so do I. We guard him with our lives." Aleta sounded as if she were waiting for a dagger to be pointed at Telemachus so she could jump in front of it.

The child doesn't know what her words mean, thought Kleea, but she nodded.

"The king took the queen in his arms one last time," she finished solemnly. "My lady tried to smile. Every woman hates to see the man she loves go off to war, and the man hates to go, but he wants to go too, and so did Odysseus. Yes, the king wanted to go. He pulled on his great plumed helmet. The queen lifted his war axe. Shuddering, she put the heavy weapon into his hands. Odysseus turned away. We heard him on the stairs, and then a noisy bustle broke out down below. When it was time, we all went down. In the courtyard, Odysseus made sacrifices to Zeus and to Athene for a safe journey. A wise man never forgets to honour the gods. Then he formed up his troop, the outer gate clanged, and they were gone. How could we guess that, nineteen years later, not one of them would have come home?"

CHAPTER TWO

THE QUEEN IS BESIEGED

Aleta loved to watch Penelope at her weaving. The great loom had been set up in the alcove at the back of the hall. That afternoon, as usual, the queen was working swiftly, pacing back and forth, shuttle flying under her skilful hands. A design of ivy leaves was growing in the cloth. Today it was ivy leaves. Tomorrow it might be part of a chariot and horses. Athene, goddess of weavers, surely guided the queen's hands. Penelope was the wisest woman in the world. She would find a way to get rid of all those horrible men. Nobody could force her to marry one of them. Even if the king never came back, they wouldn't be ruined, her grandmother must be wrong.

"Sing us a new song, Phemius," shouted one of the men. Penelope's hands stopped their rapid motion. She looked angrily at the suitors. As always, the hall

was full of them. Others took up the cry. Aleta's eyes swung around to Phemius the bard, who sat quietly in a corner, his lyre at his feet. Everybody crowded in to listen, all the men and their servants, Penelope's women, even the herdsmen. The bard picked up his lyre. Whispers of sound, clusters of notes drifted through the air. The hall grew quiet.

"I'll sing about our heroes coming home from Troy," said Phemius. "Two of them, in particular. One is King Agamemnon; the other is our own king of Ithaca, the wily Odysseus. How different are their fates! The gods gave victory to our side, but disaster followed." His fingers wandered over the strings of the lyre and found the long thrilling chords, sending shivers through Aleta's body.

Phemius raised his head and sang:

"Long was the struggle, the ten years of battle,
And weary our men when the fighting was done.
Agamemnon, the high king, set sail for his homeland,
He was the victor, the long war was won.
The voyage was easy, the gods smiled upon him,
Nothing he knew of the dark fate ahead.
Kneeling, he kissed the dear earth of Mycenae,
Little he thought that he soon would be dead.
Little he dreamed that his wife had been faithless,
Had wed with another while he had been gone.
Little he knew that fires had been lighted
To signal his false wife he soon would be home."

Aleta's eyes turned toward Penelope. What was she thinking? Her father and Queen Clytemnestra's father were brothers. The treacherous queen was Penelope's own cousin. How differently they behaved! At the loom, Penelope's quick pace had slowed. Her face was stiff and wary.

The song went on:

"Greetings, dear husband, said Queen Clytemnestra,
I see you are weary, but the water is warm.
Let me bathe you and dress you, then come to the banquet.
The king smiled and kissed her, suspecting no harm.
He put off his armour and entered the water,
She rubbed oil on his body, all slippery and wet,
Then she beckoned her lover, the traitor Aegisthus,
He lifted his spear and she picked up her net.
Agamemnon cried out, but he moved much too slowly;
His wife threw her net, and her lover his spear.
Did red wine stain the water, or was it all bloody?
His life seeped away, but his wife shed no tear."

Phemius put down his lyre slowly. Aleta shivered, thinking of the body tangled in the net, sinking into the water. Penelope was still, her face white and set. "Bravo," shouted one of the suitors.

"What about Odysseus?" cried another. "Odysseus, Odysseus," others took up the cry.

After a moment or two, Phemius picked up his lyre. Again everybody listened as he sang.

"Our great King Odysseus, Sacker of Cities,
Set sail from Troy on the wine-dark sea.
He had treasure aplenty, no reason to linger,
He longed for the babe he had held on his knee."

"The king is dead," shouted one of the men. "Put that in your song."

"Nine years have passed since Odysseus vanished;
Are his bones bleached on some desolate shore?
Does he lie with his ships in the deeps of the ocean?
Surely we'll see him on earth nevermore."

Phemius glanced at Penelope and the song died on his lips. In public, Penelope's face was guarded so that nobody could guess her thoughts. Few people had seen her weeping for her husband, but Aleta was one of those few. Her young heart ached. *The queen should not have to listen to this,* she thought, *but I can't stop it. Where is Prince Telemachus? Let him order Phemius to change his tune!* But she looked in vain. Telemachus was not in the hall.

The shuttle dropped from Penelope's hand. She pulled her scarf over her face. Phemius looked around slowly. "Sing," rose the shouts, "sing." The bard picked up his lyre again. Now he sang of King Odysseus's twelve good ships, each with its crew. None of them, not even any news of them, had ever reached Ithaca. Wasn't this enough to prove that Odysseus must be dead?

The audience clapped and cheered. "How dare you," Aleta hissed indignantly. Her wiry hands were clenched so hard that her fingernails cut into her palms. The men around her chuckled.

"Hold your tongue, little hen," one of them told her. "The king's dead. You heard it. The queen might as well believe it. Then she can marry again and let her new husband look after the kingdom. I'm ready. We're all ready." He smacked his lips.

"She'd never marry you," spat Aleta, but the men were still laughing.

"Who cares what the queen believes?" another suitor asked. "The longer she waits for a dead man, the longer the party keeps going." Everybody cheered at this.

"Let's play checkers," one invited.

"Bring your javelins," suggested another. "A flagon of mellow wine to any man who bests my throw." Several men sent servants for their javelins.

"A good offer," said Antinous, "but I vote for bows and arrows instead of javelins."

They competed in various sports until dusk. Their servants helped Penelope's people prepare and serve the nightly banquet. The suitors ate and danced and sang and went on drinking. After the meal, Penelope's disloyal women joined the men. They gossiped about Penelope's fortune and made plans for spending it. They made bad jokes. A fight started all of a sudden, and two suitors bloodied each other's noses. Aleta could have been invisible for all they noticed. At last the revellers began straggling off to sleep, some at home, others wrapped in their cloaks on the floor. A few of them were still going on with the party.

Aleta rubbed her eyes. When she was a baby, she and her mother had lived on a farm belonging to the old king Laertes, Odysseus's father. The cloth Penelope was weaving was for him, a shroud to wrap his body when he died. Aleta's nose remembered the farm: heady smells of apples, grapes trampled and fermenting, meat smoking above the hearth. Did the old king really take her on his lap and play with her? There was a feeling of scratchy whiskers against her cheek, a smell of leather, a memory of arms that held her safe. Then everything had changed. Aleta vaguely recalled bumping along on her grandmother's back during the journey to the palace. When she was tired, her head nestled into the warm space between Kleea's shoulder and neck. From time to time she would twist around to see her mother, plodding along behind.

How big it was, the palace! Vast wooden columns towered skywards at the great door. The walls stretched away forever on both sides of it. For days the frightened little girl looked for giants, sure that enormous, dangerous creatures lived in the high-ceilinged rooms. It was still the biggest building she had ever seen, but Aleta had been told often enough that it was small compared with some of the grand palaces on the mainland, and that cypress, cedar and oak were poor materials for building, compared with stone.

There were no giants, she soon discovered, only women. Indoors and out, the palace was full of them. In the upper hall they spun and wove yarn into cloth. At the river, they waded up to their knees, beating dirt out of the soiled clothes, laughing and telling stories as they worked. In the courtyard, they ground barley meal with the handmill. In the vegetable gardens and orchards, they weeded and pruned. In season, there was always a fig or a bunch of grapes for Kleea's little granddaughter, and a smile with the gift. Those were golden days, when everybody was sure King Odysseus would soon be home.

What was her mother's work? Aleta could not remember. Her grandmother had raised her. What fun they had! Sometimes Kleea boiled up a great cauldron of dye, and Aleta helped her to colour hanks of yarn or woven pieces of linen and wool. Often they went out to collect herbs or to pick wild nuts and fruit. They might climb the steep hills for chicory and lemon grass, which Kleea cut with her dark flint blade. (She left her precious bronze knife safe at home.) All summer, they picked blackberries. Kleea never scolded when Aleta's mouth was purple with their juice. Aleta never cared how much her legs got scratched. They gathered little yellow plums to dry and keep for winter, and tiny pistachio nuts that chewed down to gum in your mouth. The valley brought other joys. Aleta loved to

squish her bare feet along the muddy riverbank, trailed by her grand-mother. She always found a patch of spearmint. Then Kleea would give her a cup of mint tea, sweetened with honey, before she went to bed.

The years went by, and the king did not come back. Men began to arrive, wanting to marry the queen, a few at first, then more and more of them. Many had journeyed from far-off mainland cities or distant islands. Sons of all the important families of Ithaca came too, men who had been too young to go to war with the king or who had been kept home by their families. For three years none of them had gone home, except sometimes to sleep.

Eurymachus and Antinous reached the palace on the same day. Aleta remembered when Eurymachus had galloped into the courtyard on his black stallion. What a showoff he was! The child trailed after his servants as he swaggered into the great hall. Antinous owned vast estates on the mainland near Sparta, where Penelope's father ruled. He was the darkest man Aleta had ever seen. Although he was richer than Eurymachus, he rode a mule.

Penelope had greeted both of them politely. "Guests have always been welcome in the house of Odysseus," she told them. "I will treat you as he would do if he were here. I'm sure my husband is alive," she added firmly. "He could come home any day. I do not intend to marry again."

"You must do what's best for the country," Eurymachus argued. "It's time we had a king in Ithaca. We are gentlemen, however, we won't rush you. We will stay and let you think about it."

"By the gods, we will," Antinous chimed in. "I know your ways, lady, a man from the land where you were born. You would be comfortable with me. I'd be a good husband, and a good king too, but every one of us will tell you that. You must get to know us well before you choose. Yes, I swear by Zeus, any man who forces you will have to fight with me."

Aleta did not know the whole story, of course. Although they had promised not to rush, the suitors kept pressing Penelope to choose one of them and set a wedding date. In the beginning, the queen could have ordered them to leave. She had enough servants to force them out if they refused. But that was no way to treat your guests. Any wandering beggar might be a god in disguise, ready to reward a good host or punish a bad one. For the honour of the house, the queen's duty was to kill the finest animals and to pour out the best wine. Then more and more men arrived, and Penelope knew she could not force them to do anything.

What could she do? If Odysseus were home, he would ask the gods. Penelope called on her son Telemachus to make a sacrifice to Athene. He sacrificed a beautiful young cow and burned the thighs. The servants cooked the rest of the meat for the banquet. Athene smelled the good odour of the sacrifice. "Great goddess, send me a dream," Penelope beseeched. That night, white-robed Athene stood by the queen's bed and bent to touch the sleeper's eyelids. Penelope woke up smiling. She had a plan.

"Kleea," she ordered, "tell Mentor to change his plans for the morning. I need his advice." Soon Mentor was sitting beside her. "Arrange a meeting," she told him. "A large public meeting. I want all the suitors to be there. Their fathers too, or their uncles. Let them choose two men to speak for them. You and Telemachus will speak for me."

"Why do you want this meeting?" asked Mentor. "What are we going to say?"

"You're going to ask them to leave the palace," explained Penelope. "You will tell them and their families, in public, what I have been telling them. I do not want to get married again. I'll wait until my husband comes back, or until I'm sure he is dead."

"You know what they'll say about that," Mentor retorted. "After all these years, there would have been some news, if Odysseus was still alive. They'll say you are not acting like a queen, you're not thinking what is best for the kingdom, the kingdom needs a king. They'll tell us they are only trying to help. Forgive me, my Queen, I do not agree with them, but you know, and I know, that's what they will say."

"Yes," replied Penelope, with a smile. "So then you will tell them, or Telemachus will, that they must support me. Nobody can rule a family, let alone a kingdom, without some help from the people being ruled. It is true, though," she added quietly, "my work has got impossible since the war ended in Troy. I wish some god would tell us what has happened to Odysseus!"

"You know what people tell me," said Mentor. "If you won't marry again, you should go back to your father's house and turn the kingdom over to Telemachus."

"And if I did? How long would Telemachus last, do you think, young and powerless? Would you stay on as his advisor?"

"Of course I'd serve you always, but it would be a bad move, for me and for Telemachus. His father never handed over power to him! He's a sensible young man, and well-taught, if I do say so myself, but he is young and untried. The big families would never support him. They'd choose an

older man, one of their own. Telemachus would disappear within a month, and so would I."

"That's not a good idea, then. I didn't think it was. You are a careful man, Mentor. Over the years, you have given me good advice. What do you suggest?"

"Here's what I think," replied Mentor. "Keep the suitors here where you can see them. Entertain them, keep them busy, let them eat and drink themselves into a stupor every night. Go on that way for a few months, a year if you must, no longer. You can't afford it, and they'll get tired of it. I would advise you to set a time limit, and let them know it, when you will marry one of them if King Odysseus does not come back."

Penelope laughed. "Old friend," she said, "you and I have been thinking the same thoughts. You and Telemachus can explain my plan:

"King Laertes is an old man. One day soon his spirit will leave his body and go down to the underworld. When that day comes, he must have a funeral worthy of a king and the father of a king, and I must be ready for it. I will weave a winding cloth for his body which will do him honour. I am a skilled weaver, as you know, but this work cannot be done quickly. I keep old rams in a distant pasture for the sake of their soft wool. The shepherds must shear them and bring the long-haired fleeces for my women to spin into fine yarn. Kleea must colour it for me, her dyes are always deep and true. All this, before I can begin to weave! I'll have my great loom moved downstairs, where my unwelcome guests can see me working. They must not tell me to hurry. They must not ask how soon the shroud will be done. The day I take the finished cloth off the loom, that same day I will set the date of my wedding. Unless Odysseus comes home first, of course, or I decide after all to go back to my father's home and name Telemachus as king."

"The suitors don't think either of those things will happen," replied Mentor. "It is a good plan, Odysseus himself could not have thought of a better one. Did Athene put it into your mind?" He looked at her sharply. Penelope smiled, but did not reply. Mentor went on thoughtfully, "The suitors and their families will agree, I'm sure, since it gets them what they want and leaves them looking like gentlemen. They will like that. It's easy, too. All they need to do is wait."

Penelope was still smiling as she waved him to the door. She had not told Mentor the best part of the plan. She was going to come downstairs at night, when everybody had gone home or was asleep, and undo most of the weaving she had done that day. Years would pass before that shroud came off the loom.

ထထထ

While Aleta kept watch in the hall, the queen waited in her inner room upstairs. Moonlight streamed in through a large window. The midnight breeze was cool, but Penelope had ordered Kleea not to close the wooden shutters. The great bed beckoned invitingly, but tonight, as usual, she would work at her loom before she slept.

Penelope had aged well: her beauty was in the bones and planes of her face, the kind that lasts. Her big, dark eyes were clear and bright, and no grey showed as yet in her long black hair. She sat erect in a chair made of cypress, the dark wood inlaid with ivory, blue and gold. Kleea stood behind her. Kleea's knuckles were always more swollen and painful at night, but the hairbrush in her stiff hands moved like a caress on the queen's shining locks. Aleta's question that morning about Odysseus was still bothering her. Unless Penelope raised the subject, however, Kleea would keep her thoughts to herself.

Penelope sighed deeply. Kleea put down the hairbrush and patted her shoulder. "I can't stop thinking about that song," the queen admitted.

"Phemius has never sung so well. It's as if Apollo had lent him his lyre."

"I felt it too," Kleea agreed. "But he may be wrong about Odysseus, for all that. The gods deceive us when they want to. Dreams are often false."

"All these years," said Penelope, "I've waited for a sign. Surely Athene, or Father Zeus himself, would send a sign if my dear lord was dead. But if he is alive, why isn't he home? It has been so long, Kleea. It's hard to keep hoping, harder all the time." She paused. Downstairs, amid shouting and laughter, a bench went over with a crash. "Drunken louts!" Penelope's mood swung abruptly from wretchedness to rage. "Kleea, do you remember Odysseus wanted to leave some soldiers here?"

"I remember."

"What a fool I was, not letting him."

"You had your reasons, my lady," Kleea reassured her. "You were never a fool."

"I didn't think so, certainly. He left Mentor here. We were sure we could manage."

"Old King Laertes did what he could."

"It was easy then. Oh, not easy exactly, but there was so much good-will. Everybody wanted to help me."

"They wanted to help because they respected you. You did all the right things. When two big families got into a dispute, you listened to both sides. You didn't tell them what to do, you helped them solve it themselves."

"Women are good at that kind of thing." Penelope shrugged. "I tried to be fair. I stayed out of sight as much as I could, though. Mentor made all the announcements for me. It was better for people not to feel they were taking orders from a woman. Odysseus helped too, even though he wasn't here. I was his deputy, and everybody knew it."

"The wise Odysseus," Kleea agreed. "We were all so proud of him. Every time a messenger brought news of the war, we'd hear about another good trick. Our side would never have beaten the Trojans without him."

"Who would have thought the kingdom would fall apart so fast? I have no power these days except on my own estates, and not much even there."

"That isn't your fault."

"Everything turned upside down when the war was over. People wanted the king. They would not listen to me. They laughed at Mentor. They thought they could put off everything until Odysseus got home."

"They were wrong. You can't put off respect for law. In town, by the harbour, somebody gets a knife in the guts almost every night. The roads used to be safe everywhere in Ithaca. They aren't safe now."

Penelope was rueful. "People act as if it was all my fault. They know what I should do about it, too: remarry, so there'll be a king in Ithaca."

"Of course," said Kleea sarcastically. "It's always easy to see what somebody else ought to do. The less you know about it, the easier. All we need is a king, then we'll have blue skies and sunshine every day, full bellies and fat cattle, nothing but happiness. Any old king will do, you don't have to be particular. I can hardly wait."

Penelope threw back her head and laughed. "You are good for me, Kleea," she chuckled. They both knew it was not so simple, even if she had wanted to marry again. Once, Ithaca had really been a kingdom; now it was not. Odysseus himself, if he came home, would not easily put the pieces together. He would not easily protect himself, let alone other people.

Now Penelope waited for Aleta to tell her that all the suitors were asleep. It was getting harder to fool them. Strange stories were told, even now, of footsteps on the night stairs and dim lights where no lights should be. In the beginning, only Kleea knew the secret. Then Aleta. Now, no doubt, many of her women knew or guessed. Anyone who looked could see that the roll of finished cloth at the top of the loom never got much fatter, and the balls of warp threads wound around the clay weights at the bottom never got much smaller. Any weaver could figure it out. Nobody so far had told the suitors. Athene must be curbing the women's tongues, just as she was surely keeping the suitors asleep at night while the shuttle flew and the queen undid her work.

"Kleea, bring me wine," Penelope commanded. "We must not neglect the goddess." Kleea brought a golden cup filled with ruby wine. Penelope took it and poured out a few drops in honour of Athene. She raised the cup and drank. "Goddess of weavers," she prayed, "great goddess, help me still if you are willing."

Penelope did not know how Athene might act in the future. Gods choose for themselves how they will help or hinder mortals, but they like the sweat of human effort. Nothing angers them more than being taken for granted. Every night, Aleta would still need to watch and wait.

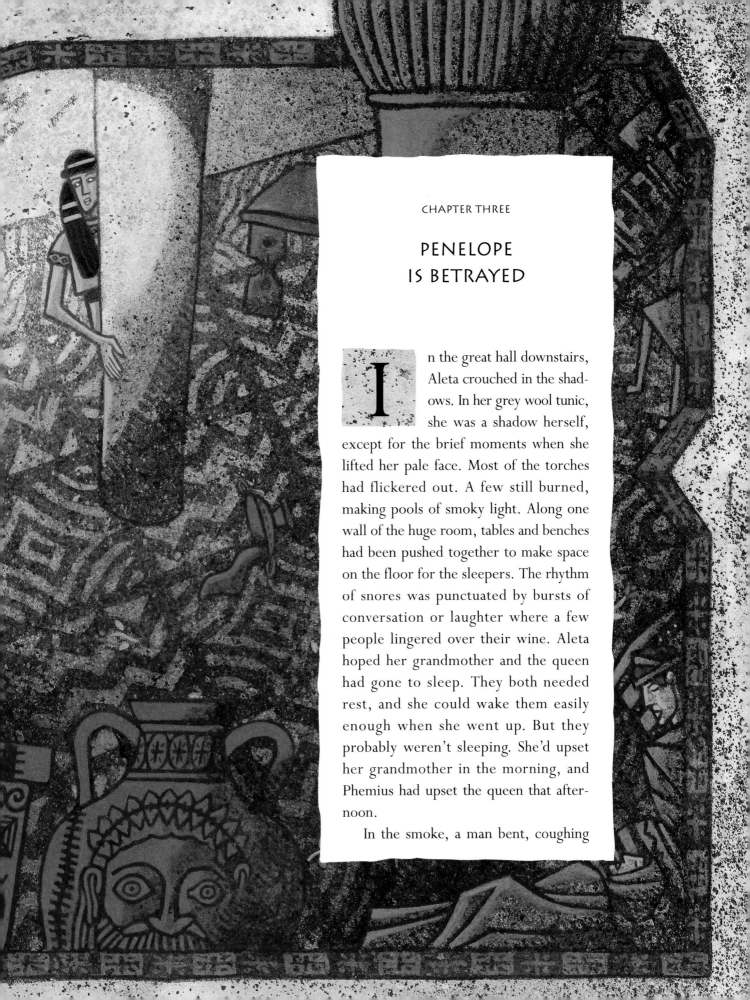

CHAPTER THREE

PENELOPE
IS BETRAYED

In the great hall downstairs, Aleta crouched in the shadows. In her grey wool tunic, she was a shadow herself, except for the brief moments when she lifted her pale face. Most of the torches had flickered out. A few still burned, making pools of smoky light. Along one wall of the huge room, tables and benches had been pushed together to make space on the floor for the sleepers. The rhythm of snores was punctuated by bursts of conversation or laughter where a few people lingered over their wine. Aleta hoped her grandmother and the queen had gone to sleep. They both needed rest, and she could wake them easily enough when she went up. But they probably weren't sleeping. She'd upset her grandmother in the morning, and Phemius had upset the queen that afternoon.

In the smoke, a man bent, coughing

and retching, his shoulders heaving. The stink of vomit prickled Aleta's nose. She heard a screech of laughter. Was that her mother's laugh? Nesta was sitting on a man's knee, the way she had been most of the evening. She was short, only a little taller than her not-yet-twelve-year-old daughter, and she was plump, though even Kleea no longer called her fat. The man had shifted his legs now and then, jiggling her into a different position. Once she half-rose, and he pulled her down again. Her right hand held a silver wine cup, which she kept raising to her mouth.

Disgusting, thought Aleta. Is Mother going to keep drinking until she pukes? Shame, the familiar feeling, engulfed her. Her mind struggled with a strange half-memory of a time when her mother might have been different, but nothing came clear and the moment passed.

Across the hall, somebody swore loudly. Aleta heard a slap, then the sound of weeping. Quietly she got to her feet, peering through the smoky dimness. Tonight was the same as every other night: a few men still yelling and laughing at the tables, a few snoring on the floor, here and there a woman on a man's knee, or shamelessly tumbled in his cloak. Well, let them, she didn't care. Her mother was as disgusting as the worst of them, however, and Aleta did care about that. Her watchful eyes narrowed again to the carved chair and the two people sitting in it, the woman on the man's lap. The man looked like a wrestler, though Aleta had never seen him wrestle. He had a bull-neck, meaty shoulders and heavy arms. Aleta gazed with dislike at his square face, topped by a fringe of carrot hair. She'd seen her mother on his lap before, but she didn't know, and didn't want to know, his name.

Nesta's left arm was around the man's thick neck. She put the silver cup on the table and leaned back to whisper in his ear. Laughing loudly, he reached around her stocky body toward the flagon of wine on the table. "Let me get it," Nesta giggled.

The couple struggled playfully over the wine. Suddenly the flagon fell over and crashed to the floor. Aleta bit back a scream. The man's big, meaty hand swung against Nesta's ear. He jerked his knees and tumbled her to the floor. He kicked her, first with one foot, then with the other. "That was your fault, you stupid woman," he grunted. "Get me more wine."

Nesta rolled heavily away from the dangerous feet. Aleta had already stepped out of her dark corner when her mother started to get up. Now the girl retreated again. Nesta swayed unsteadily, facing the man. One hand brushed at the dark red wine staining her rough grey skirt. "You drunken idiot!" she spat. "You're never going to marry Penelope. Nobody is going to marry Penelope. You are so stupid you don't even notice her weaving never gets any longer. It never will. She has been weaving the same horses and the same chariot and the same ivy every day for the last three years! If any of you stayed sober at night, you might see her slip downstairs. You might watch her rip out her work."

Aleta rushed forward. "Stop it," she gasped. Her face burned. "How could you? Mother, what have you done?"

"Aleta?" Nesta's voice was slurred. "Aleta, is that you?" She peered into the gloom. Her voice sharpened. "What are you doing here? Spying on your mother. You sly brat!" Mother and daughter faced each other.

"What's that you were saying? About Penelope?" The burly man pulled at Nesta's skirt. He lumbered to his feet. "Has she been making fools of us? I'll tell the others about that."

Aleta shuddered. Night after night, she had made sure the men were asleep before Penelope came down to undo her day's work. Was it all for nothing? "Mother didn't mean anything," she said, looking anxiously at the man. "You knocked her down. She was getting back at you, that's all, weren't you, Mother?"

Nesta looked helplessly from her daughter to her lover. She shook her head.

I must warn the queen, thought Aleta. Or Grandmother. She turned to run. "Stop her, catch that girl," shouted the big man.

Aleta ducked and dodged the two men who tried, but a tall woman caught her arm and held her. The girl spun around and looked up into golden eyes and down-turned slash of mouth. "Helen! Let me go." The woman shook her head and tightened her grip. Her sharp features were chiselled, as if cut from fine brown sandstone, polished to a shine. Aleta spat. The woman's other hand slapped the girl's mouth – hard. "Grandmother," Aleta screamed, forgetting that her grandmother was with the queen upstairs and could not possibly hear her. In the great hall, a head here and there emerged from the shadows as a startled sleeper sat up and looked around.

"Shut up," Aleta's captor hissed. Then she spoke to the others. "Nothing to worry about," she announced. "Go back to sleep." Bending Aleta's arms behind her back, Helen marched her back down the hall. "So, Castor," she asked. "What's going on?"

Aleta looked up into the man's small, mean eyes. So that was his name. Castor! Why would anybody give a god's name to this horrid man?

"Try to get away, would you," snorted Castor. His open hand cuffed Aleta's ear. Nesta stood still at his side. "I'll throw the brat in the big store-room," said Castor. "Get her out of the way till I find out what is going on. Nesta, give me the key." Slowly Nesta drew out a bronze key bigger than Aleta's hand. Castor grabbed it.

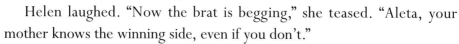

"Mother, help me," Aleta pleaded.

Helen laughed. "Now the brat is begging," she teased. "Aleta, your mother knows the winning side, even if you don't."

Nesta looked anxiously at her daughter. How often did the child ask her for anything? Her eyes stung, as if she wanted to cry, but no tears fell. "I'll keep her quiet," said Nesta slowly. "Let the girl stay with me."

"You can't keep her quiet," snapped Helen. "Nesta, try not to be such a fool." Nesta's head drooped.

"Enough," said Castor. He lifted Aleta like a sack of barley and slung her over his shoulder. "I'll come right back. Wake up Eurymachus, Helen, if he's not too far gone. We need to talk."

As he strode off with her, Aleta twisted, trying to see her mother. "Warn the queen," she pleaded, "warn her. Please, Mother, just this once." Tears stung her eyes. Hate, love, anger, shame swirled and mixed inside her. And fear. Fear, perhaps most of all. What will happen to you, Mother? What will happen to me?

Aleta knew her mother had not heard her. She was whispering and crying into Castor's back. It was no use trying to struggle; he held her ankles in a bear's grip. She got dizzy as he strode on. Finally there was a pause, a creaking noise, and she was thrown down. Pain shot through her shoulder. She gasped for breath. Behind her, a heavy door swung closed. In total darkness, Aleta heard the bolt drop into place. She thought a key was turned. Later, when the worst of the pain had passed, she felt for the latch and lifted it, but the door did not budge. She was locked in.

The room was not really cold, but the stone floor was chilling. Aleta could not stop shaking. Her teeth rattled, lower against upper, with shock, or exhaustion, or damp. Despair sat in her stomach like a stone. Queen Penelope had been so clever and so brave. Aleta had been proud of helping her. "You're like your grandmother," Penelope had told her, "you are faithful." Kleea had beckoned Aleta to her side. "We are faithful," she'd told Aleta quietly. "We are, but your mother is not. She shames us both. We have to make up for her."

Aleta had done her best, but they could never make up for Nesta now. Now, thanks to Nesta, Queen Penelope would be caught. She had promised to marry one of the suitors when her weaving was finished. That was safe enough, because the queen didn't intend to finish it. But she could not go

on secretly undoing her work. Soon the shroud would be completed. The queen would have to marry one of those drunken, noisy bullies, and it was all Nesta's fault. Aleta sobbed and shivered as the cold spread through her body. It is my fault too, she thought. I got caught, I didn't warn the queen. The girl's sobs came faster, deeper. Finally they tailed off into an exhausted sleep.

In her room upstairs, Queen Penelope paced back and forth. On the plaster wall, painted dolphins leaped and dived in a painted sea. Neither Penelope nor Kleea spared them a glance. "I'm all on edge tonight, Kleea," said the queen. "I'm out of patience. It's not only the suitors, my own people are turning traitor as well. How many of our women are loyal to the suitors and not to me?"

"Twelve of them, lady, twelve that I know about. They do not fool me. My eyes and ears are still good, and Aleta's are better. One or two more of them have not made up their mind."

"Twelve, out of fifty. And there are a hundred suitors. How can I get rid of them?"

"Kill them, my queen." Kleea's hand went to the little knife, hidden in the folds of her long tunic. "Give me the order. I can do it very quietly. You will be surprised."

Penelope laughed bitterly. "We can't kill all the traitor women, let alone the men. Could we even kill the leaders? Helen is the leader of the women, our own Helen. How about killing Helen?" Penelope raised her eyebrows. Both women thought of a different Helen, beautiful Queen Helen of Sparta, who had run away from home and started the Trojan war. Penelope stood straight and tall, like a general, thought Kleea, like a commander. "No, don't kill her, don't kill anybody without my direct order." The queen laughed, but without relaxing a muscle. "Eurycleia, daughter of Ops son of Peisenor, I forbid you to kill anybody until I say so."

Kleea's mouth twisted in a reluctant smile. "I hear you and obey, my Queen," she replied.

Penelope settled into her inlaid chair and beckoned Kleea to the stool. "I must finish my weaving," said the queen, "and then we'll need another reason to delay my marriage. I need your help and Aleta's, and I want no problems with Helen. Find the right people to watch her, Kleea." Kleea nodded. They sat in silence for a time.

"What can have happened to Aleta?" asked Penelope irritably. "Why is she so late? Time and again, I wish I had never let that child spy for us. It's dangerous. She's up half the night into the bargain. She's much too young."

"Who else can wander around without being noticed? Who else can sit in a corner and look like she's asleep? Who else can we trust?" Kleea demanded. Suddenly she was as nervous as the queen. What had happened downstairs? What was wrong? "Children grow up quickly when they must," she added, trying to make herself feel better. "Aleta knows what she's doing. Unlike her mother. Hmpf! But you're right, she is very young. I expect she has fallen asleep for once, not surprising. I'll go down, my lady, and look around."

"Wait," commanded Penelope. "Aleta has always come to tell us when everything is quiet. Perhaps she has been this late before. I want to get at my work, but I must not start before the time is right. We mustn't rush the goddess. I'll sit down again. If Aleta does not come soon, we'll go down together."

In the great hall downstairs, Helen and Nesta looked down the corridor as Castor, with Aleta over his shoulder, disappeared into the gloom. Helen turned away. Nesta had done what they told her, she always did, so why was Helen suddenly so angry with her?

The surge of anger was not new. Nesta is such a jellyfish, thought Helen. Spineless. Why do I bother with her? But the answer to that question had not changed since they were children together. Kleea's daughter was still useful to the slave woman's child, Helen wasn't finished with her yet. Besides, Nesta could be fun to be with. There was no other woman Helen could call a friend. "Let me give you some advice, Nesta," she scolded. "You're on your way to a good life with Castor. Don't throw it all away on account of your daughter. She doesn't care about you."

Nesta shuddered. "I'm not much of a mother," she said.

"Snap out of it, Nesta." Helen gave Nesta's shoulder a shake. "You did a good thing for yourself tonight. But you've never had a secret from me, not since we were children! Why didn't you tell me what Penelope was doing?"

"I wasn't certain," faltered Nesta, remembering how she had spied on the queen. What was the use of trying to keep anything secret from Helen? Even when they were children, Helen always knew when she was lying, and she was always furious. Back then Helen had been as lonely as Nesta, but she was always sharp. Could Nesta get away with telling her only part of the story? She plowed on, "Mother talked in her sleep one night, that's what put me onto it. I was going to tell you, tomorrow, the next day for sure. I was scared, Helen. Who am I beside my mother and the queen?" The trembling was all through her. "I never meant to say anything to Castor. He kicked me hard tonight, and I just burst out with it."

Helen laughed grimly. "I'm always the one who knows everything," she said. "Except this time. Eurymachus should have heard it from me. If you want to be my friend, Nesta, don't be so soft."

Helen certainly was not soft. Everything about her was sharp: a sharp nose for smelling out plots, sharp ears for hearing threats, sharp eyes to see a slight, whether or not intended, sharp chin and sharp elbows for thrusting other people aside, and a sharp mind for planning. Only her mouth was not sharp. It was full and pouty, with an out-thrust underlip. Nesta knew perfectly well why she hadn't told Helen about the night unweaving: Helen would tell Eurymachus, and Kleea would know somehow, she always knew when it was Nesta's fault. Nesta had enough trouble with Kleea already.

Helen tapped her briskly on the shoulder. "Nesta," she warned, "don't forget our plans. Eurymachus for me and Castor for you. They need us, and they know it. We've got to keep it that way. When Eurymachus leaves this palace, he'll take me to run his household and nurse his sons, like your mother does here."

"Don't count on me. I'm not my mother, and I never will be," said Nesta dully. "You can't change your fate."

"You can't know your fate either," Helen snapped back. "Nesta, I'll keep on until it sinks in. If I need your help, you'd better be ready. I am not staying here all my life! Odysseus, Sacker of Cities! People say it as if it was a great thing. As if they knew! Odysseus burned my father's city and carried off my mother as his slave." Helen's gold eyes burned with rage. Nesta drew back. "I was just a baby, but Mother never let me forget. You heard her yourself, more than once. I am Helen, daughter of Erastos son of Medon. My mother's mother came from far-off Egypt. I was born a lady. My mother hated Odysseus. She hated his wife and son, and so do I. Some day I'll dance on their graves, and if my hand puts them there, so much the better." Helen's voice was getting calmer. "Now come and help our friends get ready to confront Penelope," she added. Nesta nodded soothingly. The sharp tip of Helen's tongue ran greedily over her lower lip.

Helen crossed the hall and knelt beside a sleeper. She pulled a blue cloak away from a face that would have been handsome except for an oversize chin. "Wake up, Eurymachus," she said. She tickled the man with the fur that trimmed his cloak. He snorted and rolled over. Castor, back from the storeroom where he had dumped Aleta, pushed her aside and shook the sleeper roughly, then pulled him up to sit with his back against the wall. He squatted to tell his story. After a minute or two, Eurymachus stood up, his face crimson with rage.

Unlike the other suitors, Eurymachus and Antinous were impatient for the party to end. They expected Penelope to marry one of them. Eurymachus wanted her to marry him before all her wealth had been eaten and drunk up. She had been a good host long enough. Eurymachus felt as if it was his money that was being wasted. He was sure Antinous felt the same way. The money did not belong to either of them, of course, but as soon as Penelope finished her weaving and set her wedding date, that would change.

Antinous did not care about Penelope's money, Eurymachus was wrong about that. He wanted Penelope to marry him before she got too old to have more children. He wanted to be king of Ithaca, but he wanted to marry Penelope even more. She was wise and beautiful and loyal, more than any other woman he could imagine. Her father's kingdom wasn't far from his own great lands. Sometimes he dreamed that their son, his and Penelope's, would one day rule in Sparta. The queen liked him, Antinous was sure. He was glad they'd all agreed to give her time. No doubt she would choose him as soon as her weaving was finished, and that could hardly take much longer. Antinous knew Penelope could not make a better choice.

Sometimes Eurymachus thought about forcing Penelope to marry him right away, but he did not want a fight with Antinous. They had agreed that Penelope could finish weaving the shroud. Then she would marry him. Eurymachus came from the most important family in Ithaca. The other big families would support him. She would never marry somebody from far away. But Penelope herself had broken their agreement, if Castor was right. Now the other sleepers, rubbing their eyes and shaking their heads, gathered round. Eurymachus told the others about Penelope's night work.

Antinous shook his head. "It's hard to believe she'd play such a trick on us," he admitted. "I never suspected a thing."

"Makes you feel really stupid, doesn't it," Castor complained. "I even woke up once and saw her, like a shadow, at that loom. I thought it was a dream, never thought another thing about it."

"We weren't stupid," Eurymachus protested. "She was clever, but we all know she's a clever woman. Why would we pay attention to her weaving? That's women's work. Who cares what women do? She knew we would not check up on her, that's how she tricked us all this time." We're important men, he told himself; now everybody is going to laugh at us. His nostrils were white with rage. His right fist clenched itself and came up to beat rhythmically against his open palm. Eurymachus liked his dignity.

Antinous shrugged. "Does it matter? She's broken her agreement. We'll catch her." He looked round at the angry faces. "Tonight, before somebody warns her. We will tell the world what she has been doing." Everybody nodded. "We'll pretend to be sleeping. Let her go to the loom and work for a while," he added. "I'll give the sign, and we can all close in."

"Me first," spluttered Eurymachus.

Grimly, the men lay down again. The queen's great loom towered, untended, in the alcove at the far end of the hall. The dark frame looked like a shadow against the white plastered wall. The massive loom dwarfed the door beside it which hid the stairs leading to the women's quarters and to Penelope's inner room. Nesta had not gone to hide with the suitors, but she didn't dare go upstairs. She lay unhappily on the floor, pretending to be asleep. She was completely sober now. A fold of her cloak concealed her face.

The watchers did not have long to wait. Soundlessly, the small door opened. Penelope glided in, followed by Kleea. Nesta had feared this, and her throat tightened. With all her heart, she wished her mother had not come. The old woman carried a torch and fitted it into a holder on the wall. She crept into the hall a little way and looked around, then drifted back again. She must have nodded or made some other sign of safety, for Penelope took the shuttle and started to work the threads. With quick, soft steps she moved back and forth, back and forth, undoing the work she had done that day. Kleea kept peering into the hall, but nobody stirred. There were no snores. Except for the small sounds of the loom and the weaver's footsteps, it was dead silent. Nesta felt a scream or a groan, some kind of loud noise, building up inside her. Could she keep quiet? For how long?

When Antinous gave his yell, Nesta echoed it. Her mother swept up the torch. Penelope dropped her shuttle and took two quick steps toward the little door. "Stop," cried Eurymachus. The men crowded into the small alcove. Penelope gathered her dignity and turned to face them, tall and proud. Old Kleea stood behind the queen, on her right. Behind them, Nesta backed up against the wall. The latch of the upstairs door dug into her back, and she moved crabwise, supporting herself, until she stood beside it.

"Queen Penelope, you have been very clever," Eurymachus began. "You told us you had to weave a winding sheet for your husband's father. Lord Laertes is very old, you said. When death comes for him, I must be ready. That's what you told us! You had your loom brought down so that we could see you at your work. You swore by the goddess Athene herself that you would choose a new husband when the shroud was done."

Antinous broke in, "We could have pressed you to marry quickly, but we waited. We trusted you. We honoured you because you respected the old king. Once in a while, it seemed you were taking a long time, a skilled weaver like you," he continued. "But I thought, Lord Laertes has been a king in his time, and the father of a king. He retired to his farm years ago, but he is still an important man, there should be a special cloth to wrap him when he is lowered into his grave. I never suspected this!"

"And all the time, you were tricking us," roared Eurymachus. Rage thickened his voice. "Not any more, my lady." Penelope raised her eyebrows, and Eurymachus lost control entirely. "Lady, ha!" he snorted. "Cheat! Fake! Fraud! Hypocrite! Liar!" He lunged at Penelope. The queen did not move or speak. Eurymachus's badly aimed fist caught Kleea's shoulder, spinning her back against the wall. Antinous and Castor grabbed him, one on each side. The enraged man threw off Antinous, but only for a moment, then he was held again. All three men faced Penelope, slippery with sweat.

"Terrible," puffed Antinous. "This is terrible. But it's your fault, lady. You need a husband."

"You?" Penelope's eyes glittered. "Never. You can apologize tomorrow. Then all of you can leave." She turned. Nesta still slumped against the wall by the door, dizzy with terror, hiding her face.

"I will not leave," Eurymachus shouted, "not until you marry me."

"Open the door, Kleea," ordered Penelope. "We're going to bed." The queen's angry hand shot out to the woman beside the door and threw aside her cloak. Penelope drew a sharp breath, but showed no other sign of shock. Kleea gasped as if she had been hit.

"Nesta." Kleea's voice was bitter. "My own daughter. You told them about this, didn't you. Traitor," she spat. Nesta made no reply, but her face was white and miserable. Kleea reached awkwardly to open the door. She bolted it on the other side behind Penelope and herself.

In the bedchamber, Kleea shuddered as she combed out the queen's long black hair. Her tears fell as she knelt to wash Penelope's feet.

Penelope stroked Kleea's shoulder. "We'll talk about Nesta tomorrow," she said gently. "Keep your place at my door tonight, old friend. Sleep if you can. After tonight, I'll need your help more than ever."

CHAPTER FOUR

THE SEARCH FOR ODYSSEUS

P enelope woke suddenly next morning, her ears full of an odd whirring sound. What could it be? Quietly, she opened her eyes. Kleea stood beside the open window, looking down at the knife in her hand. Its gold and silver hilt glittered in the bright morning sun. She lifted her arm and stabbed the air, as if the bronze blade was slicing into human flesh. That was the sound, the knife hissing through the air.

"Are you forgetting my orders so soon?" Penelope's voice was firm. "Who are you planning to kill?"

"Nesta, of course." Kleea looked embarrassed and defiant at the same time.

"Because she told the suitors I undo my weaving?"

"She betrayed you."

"I'm not pleased, but they were bound to find out sometime. For the moment, it's even a relief. I am tired of trickery,

Kleea. How lucky that Eurymachus put himself in the wrong last night. Athene is still looking after me."

"My daughter gave you to your enemies. After all you've done for her. She brings me nothing but shame. I brought her into the world. Who has more right to send her out of it?"

"Stop it, Kleea," ordered Penelope. "Kill your own child? The furies would surely destroy you. Nesta isn't worth it. If she has betrayed me, then I will decide how and when she will be punished. Put down that knife, Kleea. She is Aleta's mother. Think about your granddaughter. And on that subject, Kleea, where is the child? Aleta never did turn up last night, did she. I'm surprised you're not off looking for her."

The wild light faded from Kleea's eyes. At last she nodded. "Forgive me," she begged. "Your enemies attacked you last night in my presence, and I had to stand by and do nothing."

"True," agreed Penelope. "There was nothing you could do. Kleea, put down the knife."

"It weighed on me. That, as well as Nesta." Kleea shuddered. "I lay in bed for hours before Aleta even entered my mind. Then I tried to get up and search for her and had to lie down again. I was sick and dizzy. At last the kind gods closed my eyes in sleep. This morning everything but Nesta had vanished from my mind. How could I forget about the child? The furies will be after me if she has been hurt. I'll go now, my lady, with your permission." She looked in surprise at the knife in her hand. Slowly, she put it down.

"Start with Nesta," Penelope said firmly, hiding her own remorse and concern. "Mentor will be arriving soon, and I need to get ready for him. I'll brush my own hair for a change." Her hair still looked black and glossy in the sunlight, though not as shiny as when Odysseus went away. Kleea's footsteps faded as the old woman hurried down the stairs.

Downstairs, Nesta bent over a table near the hearth. She was shaping little honeycakes. "Cakes for Castor, I suppose," Kleea's words dripped acid. Nesta cowered away from her mother. When the blow she was waiting for did not come, she lifted her head a little. Contempt blazed in Kleea's face. "I'm ashamed of you, again," she raged. "And surprised, though I don't know why I should be. What have you ever done to make me proud? Do you know where your daughter can be found?"

"They locked her up last night." Nesta's voice was flat. "She was in the hall. She tried to get me in trouble with Castor."

"Did she, now. Were you frightened?" Kleea's sarcasm turned to icy rage. "Get her released, Nesta. Bring her to the queen's room. Use your influence with your friends."

"*My* influence?" Nesta laughed bitterly, but she turned and went.

In the dark room, Aleta sat on cold stone with her back against wood. Her tongue was swollen. She had needed to urinate for so long that she had gone past discomfort and pain. Now her whole lower body was cramped. When the light changed, when she realized that the door was actually opening, she wanted to jump to her feet and run, dodging past whoever was there. Impossible. She could not move. Her voice at last was a surprised croak. "Mother?"

"Get up, Aleta." Nesta spoke briskly. "Here." She pulled Aleta up, catching the girl as she swayed on numb feet. "Come along, lean on me. We'll get you cleaned up. Your grandmother and the queen are waiting."

She was partly right. Kleea was waiting, but Penelope was deep in discussion with Mentor and impatient for Telemachus to arrive. Mentor was moving more slowly every day. He was talking more slowly. He seemed to be thinking more slowly. His left hand absentmindedly scratched his ear.

"I'm tired, my lady," he apologized. Penelope started. It was almost as if he had heard her thoughts! "I work harder than ever, but nothing gets settled. I meet with parties to a dispute. We talk. Sometimes they make an agreement, but then it falls apart again. I've been trying to get a troop together to clean up the road to the harbour, get rid of the robbers. It's a disgrace. I get a few men together, but not enough, and by the time more arrive, others have drifted off. Everything goes like that." He shook his head.

"You speak for me," Penelope reminded him, "and through me, for Odysseus. Doesn't that mean anything?"

Mentor bowed his head. "I am ashamed," he said. "I do the best I can. 'You can't speak for Odysseus, he's dead,' they tell me. 'The queen can't speak for a dead husband, either.' "

"They are not happy with either of us, these days," replied the queen. "I wish I could help you, Mentor, but I spend all my time and energy right here, trying to keep my suitors from ruining me and my son." She paused for a moment. "The people would listen to Odysseus," she added. There was a knock on the door, and Telemachus came in.

"By Zeus and by Athene too, I wish Odysseus was here," exclaimed Mentor. He shook his head.

Telemachus sat down. He nodded to Mentor and exchanged a loving smile with his mother. "Some days I'm certain my father is alive," he told them, "other days I'm just as sure he must be dead. We want him to be alive, so we tell ourselves he must be alive. It doesn't mean anything." He put a hand on his mother's shoulder. "You used to tell stories about how my father went to war. How long did it take him to reach Troy with all his men?"

"About three months, I'd say," replied Penelope.

"That's about right," agreed Mentor, "including the weeks while the whole Greek force sat by the seashore waiting for the wind. Three months, four at the outside."

"It's nine years since the fall of Troy," said Telemachus quietly. "Nine years, when the voyage home should have taken four months at the most?" He looked at his mother's face. Lines of age and sadness showed in the morning light. "I'm so sorry, Mother," he said.

"Would you rather we talked about something else?" asked Mentor. "Are your suitors behaving any better? Kleea tells me more of your maids are going over to them."

Penelope shook her head. "Let's not change the subject," she said. "I know how long it has been since Troy was burned. The years have not slipped by without my noticing. Time passes and things change, whatever our wish may be."

"All the same," said Mentor eagerly, "Odysseus may not be dead. An ogre might have seized him. Some enchantress might have made him her prisoner."

"More likely he offended one of the gods," retorted Penelope. "When his temper was up, sometimes he forgot about common sense." She looked thoughtfully at her son. "Mentor," she said, "you and I have ruled Ithaca for nearly twenty years. Look at Telemachus here. You have taught him well. He isn't a boy any longer." It was true. Her son did not back away from facts, even if they were unpleasant. We've brought him up to be a king, thought Penelope, even though his father wasn't here. She smiled.

Telemachus slid forward to the edge of his chair. Surely his mother would approve of his plan! All the same, he would keep quiet until Mentor left.

∞∞∞

For Aleta, the next half-hour passed in a blur. The girl was vaguely aware of a chamber pot, cold water on her face, a comb pulled painfully through her tangled hair. Nesta half-carried her up the stairs. Suddenly Kleea was there, taking Aleta's other arm, and her mother disappeared. Aleta found herself on a bench in the queen's room, not quite knowing how she got there. Penelope patted her shoulder. "That's a relief," she said.

Nesta reappeared with water, honeycakes and figs. She turned to leave, but Aleta, on impulse, caught at her tunic. Nesta looked at the queen.

"May I come back later?" she asked, with a gesture toward Aleta. "Just to see how she is." Penelope nodded.

Aleta sipped. Her mother had poured wine into the water, more than Aleta had ever drunk before. She was sitting across from the dolphin wall in the queen's room, and she felt as if the dolphins were moving and she was moving with them. Why was she so dizzy? Was it the wine, or the memory of her mother finding her? How strange! Her grandmother had often kissed away cuts and bruises, but not her mother, not that she could remember. But then, she could not remember everything. Now her grandmother stood behind the queen, teasing Penelope's long black hair into elaborate swirls, and paid no attention to her at all. Between sips, Aleta chewed at a fig or tore off another piece of cake.

Prince Telemachus was the only other person in the room. He was arguing furiously with his mother. It sounded as if he was planning a journey. Aleta was shocked. He was wrong twice over: wrong to argue and wrong to want to go away. How could he even think of it? The queen's face was white.

"I can't forbid you to go," Penelope admitted. "But you would be safer here." Oh-oh, thought Aleta, that was the wrong thing to say! Telemachus flushed angrily. "I'd be safer too," Penelope added quickly. "The suitors will hardly kill you here. They couldn't keep it secret. Even their own families would hardly dare to protect them. They would be condemned. But they want you dead, make no mistake about it. If they could set an ambush away from here, if they could kill you and make it look like an attack by thieves or pirates, that would suit them perfectly. Why would I hold out any longer, if you were dead?"

Telemachus stood up abruptly, pushing back the inlaid chair. "If that's the way they think, they're wrong," he said. "You believe my father is alive. With all my heart, I hope you're right. The suitors think he is dead. Let them think so. Mother, you listened to me an hour ago. What has changed? We need news of Odysseus. It's doubly urgent, now that the suitors know how you've tricked them with your weaving. Even if I don't find my father, I'll get news."

"I'm afraid for you." Penelope shivered as if her bones were cold. Aleta felt like crying.

Telemachus cleared his throat a couple of times. "I must go," he said at last. "Listen, Mother." He lowered his voice. "Mentor talked to me last week. This journey was his plan. But when I saw Mentor the very next day, he did not seem to know what I was talking about. Isn't that strange? It is as if two Mentors have been talking to me. The other one looks exactly like Mentor, same grey curls and beard, same weatherbeaten face, same hairy mole on his chin. He talks with Mentor's voice, but he is not Mentor, truly. He was facing the harbour, talking about one or two men who might lend me a ship, and then he turned and looked right at me. 'This journey is the will of the gods,' he declared. His eyes were shining arrows, holding me. I knew it was one of the gods who spoke. Mother, this *is* the will of the gods. I've never been more certain about anything in my life."

"That's what your father said when he went off to Troy."

"Wasn't he right?"

"How do I know? He has not come back to tell me. I'm very angry with Mentor. He has no right to say things like that without talking to me."

"I've been trying to tell you, Mother, it was not Mentor. Mentor knows nothing about it, you can ask him yourself."

"Believe me, I will ask him. Telemachus, the suitors will try to kill you if you go away. 'Aha,' they'll say, 'look at Telemachus, his mother can't keep him home any more. First thing we know he'll be telling everybody he is old enough to be king. We had better get rid of him while we have the chance!' Think, Telemachus! The suitors behave like animals. Like animals, they have a nose for danger. You are a danger to them."

"Come now, Mother." Telemachus did not believe her. "I'm simply a nuisance to those bullies. I get angry at them, feasting on our animals, drinking our wine, stealing our people's loyalty. They don't like me. They'd be happy if I had an accident, but they would not murder me."

"Yes, they would." Nesta, standing by the door, spoke quietly. Even Aleta had not heard her come back in. Everybody was startled. Kleea got that closed, watchful look. She always looked like that when Nesta shamed her.

"Tell us." Penelope was quiet too.

"They plan your death, Telemachus," Nesta began.

"Why should we believe *you*?" Kleea had put her knife away, but its edge was in her voice. Nesta's mouth tightened. The room was silent.

"Go on, Nesta," commanded Penelope. "Tell us about these plans."

Nesta raised her eyes. "It's talk, more than plans," her soft voice admitted. "If the prince goes to see his grandfather, what is the best place for two or three killers to hide? Can they provoke Telemachus so that he decides to leave the island? If he leaves, who has the best ship to attack him? Where should it lie in wait?"

"I don't believe you." Telemachus was shocked.

His mother shook her head. "Who is behind this talk?" she asked sharply. Nesta shrugged her shoulders. "Do they all talk the same way?"

"No, they don't." Nesta frowned as she tried to get it clear in her mind. Castor and Eurymachus did the most talking, but she didn't want to say so. Why couldn't she keep her mouth shut? Now she had to say something; the queen was waiting. "Antinous doesn't like it," she said at last. "He told Eurymachus he'd warn the boy if he had to. 'Is that the way to a mother's heart,' he asked, 'to kill her son?' "

"Now you tell us, now." Kleea's throat was thick with rage.

"Silence," commanded the queen. Her dark eyes never left Nesta's face. "Are they divided then? Would Antinous help me?"

Nesta shook her head. "If he was sure you were going to marry him, maybe," she offered. "But I don't think so."

"I don't either," agreed Penelope grimly. "Antinous doesn't mean everything he says. He is a careful man. And I am a careful woman. Should I believe you? Why tell us about this now, after what you did last night? Are you trying to change sides again?"

"No," shouted Nesta. "I don't know," she added miserably. "Don't count on anything. You know me, I do what's easy. I shame you, I disgrace you, I'm a coward. But they say they will kill Telemachus unless you marry one of them."

Penelope looked directly at Nesta. "Leave us, Nesta," she commanded. "Be a coward, since you must. Cowards have their uses. But understand me well, I have no use for treachery." The others sat unmoving until the door had closed. "Come and sit with us, Aleta," Penelope beckoned.

Aleta burrowed against her grandmother. Always afterwards, when she imagined how grand and terrible the goddess Athene would look, she remembered how the queen looked then.

"Do you believe her?" Penelope asked Kleea.

"I wish I didn't," Kleea shivered, "but I do."

"It's no more than I expected," Penelope nodded. "I won't count on Nesta, but perhaps she will tell us more. Perhaps she is sorry about last night. Telemachus, I don't want you to be bait for those suitors."

"I can think of one way to stop that," said Kleea abruptly, "but I don't like it." Penelope raised her eyebrows. "Should you marry one of the brutes?" asked Kleea. "Antinous, perhaps? To save your son?"

"No," growled Telemachus.

"No." Penelope was impatient. "I'd hate it, and it would be no help. Antinous is smoother than the others, I grant you, but he is not really any different. Suppose I do marry one of them. He uses me to become king. Now he has power and authority. But Telemachus, alive, will always be a danger to him. How long do you think the son of King Odysseus and Queen Penelope would live?"

Telemachus gritted his teeth. Kleea nodded. "What else can we do?"

"I could give up. That is another choice. I could go back to my father and say, 'Give me another dowry, Father, and find me another husband.' Wouldn't he be delighted!" The queen gave a loud and undignified snort. "If you were a little older, Telemachus, I'd turn the kingdom over to you. But you would need support from the important families, and you would not get it, not while they hope one of their sons will marry me." The queen sat very straight, but her shoulders looked tired.

Telemachus took her hand gently. "I'm sure you're right, Mother." His voice was tender. "But this settles it, we must have news of my father, and I must get it."

"If you can get away safely, with a crew we can trust, it is a better idea than I thought at first. I haven't given it a chance to settle in my mind. Do you truly believe one of the gods is helping you?"

"Truly, Mother. I'll be looked after. But I am worried about you," Telemachus continued. "Would the suitors try to force you to marry one of them after I leave? Would they go that far?"

Penelope shook her head. "I think not," she said. "It's different if I give in and choose one of them, the way they want me to do. Then nobody will blame them for eating our food and drinking our wine and corrupting our people. It would be very different if Odysseus came back, or if his son was king," she mused. "Odysseus could demand repayment from the men and from their families for all the damage they've done here, and that would just be the beginning. I hope I'm right about all this," she added. But the doubt, if there had been doubt, vanished at once. "Now, Telemachus," she said briskly, "what are your plans? You should get away quickly."

"You'll have to pretend you don't know about it," the young man replied. "Wouldn't it be better if I don't tell you? Then you can be surprised along with our enemies. You won't have to pretend."

"Nonsense," snapped his mother. "I want to know where you're going, and when, and how."

Telemachus nodded. "Noemon is lending his ship for as long as I need it. Mentor – the god-Mentor – is rounding up twenty men to row her. I'll go to Pylos first." Telemachus pursed his lips in a sudden whistle. "By the gods, Kleea, if you can get my supplies together today, I can likely put to sea tonight. Can you still work miracles?"

Kleea's bent back straightened, as if years had been lifted from her shoulders. She patted Telemachus's arm. "There's nothing I couldn't do for you, Telemachus, and well you know it, and have known since you were a baby. Besides, Aleta will help me. Food, wine, a new cloak, what else do you want?"

"I'll look after my own hunting gear and armour. Give me two or three gold and silver cups and a few other things, small but precious. There's no extra space in the boat, but I need a few rich gifts."

"The little knife inlaid with ivory and gold," said Penelope, "take that. Hephaestus could have made it, it's so beautiful. The helmet made of boars' teeth, the mate to the one your father took to war, that's a fine gift. Kleea, give him a necklace of amber beads, and one of amethysts, from my jewel box. You've never been far from home, Telemachus. You'll visit rich kingdoms, where huge herds of cattle get fat on meadows that stretch as far as you can see. You'll sleep in palaces where the great hall alone is as big as our whole house. We think this is a big place, and it is, there's not another like it in the whole of Ithaca, but King Menelaus of Sparta has a palace three times this size, and built of brick and stone, not wood. Ithaca is a rough land, all rocks and rivers and wooded slopes, better for goats or sheep than fat cattle or swift horses. You're the son of Odysseus and the grandson of Laertes, all the same. I want you to be a credit to your family."

"The son of Queen Penelope, too." Aleta's voice trembled. Everybody smiled.

"You have trained me well, Mother," said Telemachus. "I won't disgrace you. It is time for me to see some of these rich places and meet the people who rule them. Don't try to tell me any other place is more beautiful than Ithaca, though. I would not believe you."

"No," smiled Penelope, "there's no land more beautiful or more dear to us. Treasure it in your heart."

Aleta lifted a sad little face. "I wish you didn't have to go."

"Don't look like that, Aleta," complained Telemachus, "as if you'd lost your last best friend. Remember, I'm going to find my father so we can get rid of our enemies."

"You'll miss our birthday," said Aleta, who had been thinking about this for some time. "The first birthday since Mother and I came here from the farm that you and I won't look at the stars together. Your journey will not be over in a month."

Telemachus laughed. "We'll have other birthdays," he said lightly. "Good ones, too, and other times to look at our stars. The gods are looking after us, I'm sure of it." The tall young man touched the forlorn little shoulder.

Kleea stood up. "Come and help me, Aleta," she said. "We have work to do."

"Can you manage, Kleea?" asked Penelope. "You and Aleta? I hope you can. The fewer people who know this secret, the better." Kleea nodded.

"I'm off to the harbour," Telemachus announced. "I'll be back when my ship and crew are ready."

Aleta followed her grandmother down the stairs and across the great hall into a dark corridor. Now the girl hung back. Her grandmother was almost out of sight by the time she gathered her courage and ran after her, catching up in front of a huge old wooden door. The door was formed from wide planks. A bolt as well as a lock protected the room within.

Aleta stumbled. She heard her grandmother's voice as if from a great distance. "Sit down, Aleta. Put your head down. Are you going to faint?"

Aleta shook her head without looking up. "I'm all right," she said. "What is this room?"

"Ah," replied Kleea. "This is the great storeroom. It holds the king's treasure. You've been everywhere else in the palace, I expect – except for the men's quarters, of course." She laughed. "Well, my girl, you'll be amazed. Bring me a torch. Now, where's my key?"

Aleta brought the torch. She knew the women's quarters and the great hall very well, but in all her years until last night she had not been in this corridor. Last night she had seen it upside down, bumping against Castor's back. She watched while her grandmother searched for the key.

"What a time to lose it, when there's so much to do," complained the old woman. At last she sat on the floor and put her head on her knees. "Keep quiet, Aleta," she said. "I have served Athene well, like all who love Odysseus. I must ask the goddess for a dream to tell me where I have put the key."

Aleta got up quietly and went to look for Nesta. How many keys could there be to this room? Somebody had one last night. "Grandmother can't find the key to the storeroom, Mother," said the girl. "She is waiting for a sign from Athene, and it may be the goddess has sent me to you. Was it grandmother's key that Castor used last night?"

"I borrowed it," grumbled Nesta, "and I wish I hadn't. Castor likes good wine, and that's where the best wine is kept. You're too smart, Aleta. I've borrowed that key a time or two, but it's always been easy enough to put it back. Mother never missed it. Don't look at me like that, girl. We never took much of anything except some wine and oil. Castor was a fool last night, locking you in there. Now I'm in worse trouble, and all because of your spying. All right, clever daughter, Castor has that key. I'll get it back. Stay here; the less he sees of you the better."

Aleta did not have long to wait. Soon her mother returned, and the

bronze key lay heavy and cold in the girl's hand. "Keep me out of it if you can," asked Nesta, looking down at Aleta's troubled face. "On second thought, tell your grandmother all about it if you want, what's the difference? She won't be surprised."

Aleta turned into the corridor more easily this time and sat down again beside Kleea. She held out the key. Her grandmother's eyebrows rose. The old grey eyes raked the young woman. Aleta knew that her grandmother guessed exactly what had happened. Kleea shook her head in disgust. She got up awkwardly and unlocked the door.

"This is where they locked me up last night," whispered Aleta.

"They have no respect," replied Kleea bitterly. "Let's see what's missing. Come in, child. You don't have to be afraid."

With two torches fixed to the walls, the shadows retreated. Aleta gasped. Such a room! She had never seen anything like it. From the stone floor to the high rafters, it gleamed with gold and silver and bronze: chairs, armour, shields and spear tips winked and blinked in the flickering light. Huge chests were piled up, one on top of another. One wall was lined with two-handled wine jars higher than her head, another with huge jars of sweet-smelling oil. Sacks of costly grain were heaped ceiling-high. Curious, Aleta took one of the torches over to a pile of wooden chests. Yes, this was where she had sat last night, not leaning against a wall. In the whole cavernous room, there was no bare wall.

Meanwhile, Kleea too had been inspecting. Now she turned to Aleta. "Thieves have been here," said the old woman grimly, "but not often and not for long, as far as I can tell. It will not happen again. Are you ready for work? Bring me twelve flagons for wine, and make sure the stoppers are good. Ten strong leather bags for grain. I'll get the gold and silver cups. There's a bowl of cypress wood, inlaid with silver dolphins, I must show it to you, and a golden griffin. Look here, Aleta, the king's chariot! It looked better with its wheels attached." The body of the chariot was sitting on the floor. The tall wheels stood behind it.

"Why didn't the king take it with him?" asked Aleta curiously. She ran her hands over the crimson paint. Ivory inlays of horses looked ready to gallop off the sides!

"He loved this chariot, but he wouldn't take it," replied Kleea. "The one he took was lighter. I remember, it was inlaid with men's figures in gold. A chariot fit for our king! But Odysseus never liked to fight from a chariot," she added. "He took it, but like as not it never got into battle. We're wasting time, Aleta. Get those flagons."

Aleta and Kleea worked well together, dipping out wine and barley-meal. Kleea packed the precious cups in wool. Aleta stuffed two new cloaks into a leather satchel. From a small chest that she unlocked with a tiny golden key, Kleea took two bronze pins with crystal heads. She worked a pin into the collar of each cloak. She locked the casket again and put the key carefully away. "That's everything I can think of," she nodded. "Telemachus will have to find a way to get it out. Come, Aleta." Aleta opened the huge door. The torches were burning low, but she set them back into holders in the corridor.

Kleea's face contorted suddenly in pain, and her right hand went to her chest.

"What's wrong?" Terror struck at Aleta. "Sit down, Grandmother. I'll get somebody."

"No, too dangerous." Kleea's voice was sharp and urgent. She leaned against Aleta, breathing deep and slow. "Give me a moment, I'll be fine." Aleta braced herself against the wall. "We'll go now," said Kleea. "Slowly. Yes, child, help me. When we reach the hall we can sit down."

In the great hall, Aleta settled her grandmother on a carved chair against the wall. "I don't like this," muttered Kleea. "We are too close to that passage. Somebody's going to wonder what we have been doing."

"I'll bring water," said Aleta.

"Bread and cheese too," Kleea suggested. "We need to eat."

They munched and gulped. "I'm getting old." Kleea's voice was tired. "Twenty years ago, ten years even, that would have been easy."

Kleea's eyes weren't as sharp as they had been, but the scene in the hall was no different that day from any other, as far as she could see. Men and women bustled about, getting ready for that night's banquet. Most of the suitors had brought servants to look after them. These men helped the women of Penelope's household to prepare for the party. Like their masters, they liked to eat and drink. Now, they joked as they scrubbed the tables and chairs and pulled them into place. In the alcove at the far end, Penelope paced evenly back and forth at her loom. Now her weaving would not be undone. Women with huge baskets went from table to table, putting out fresh bread. Nesta was one of them. She walked down the nearest row of tables. Aleta watched her, but her mother moved quickly and kept her eyes down. Another woman did not trouble to hide her gaze. "Helen," Kleea muttered. "I want to go outside, Aleta."

"Lean on me, Grandmother," urged Aleta, but Kleea didn't lean. Her steps were quick and sure, as usual. Helen could have spoken to them, Aleta's glance caught her tawny eyes as they passed. It was her sharp look, disconcerting. Then they were past the danger, if it was a danger, and out of Helen's sight.

Down at the harbour, Telemachus found his ship caulked and painted. Mentor beckoned him aboard – Mentor or whatever bright-eyed god had borrowed Mentor's form. "She's in perfect shape, ready to go any time," he called. "Come and inspect her. Your crew are on the way, twenty loyal men. They'll row you to Pylos and anywhere else you choose. No doubt you'll hear about your father soon."

"Dear friend, I can't find the right words to thank you," stammered Telemachus. "You have worked wonders." His eyes checked the sturdy ship from prow to stern: the fir mast was stepped; the white sail lay ready to hoist with braided oxhide ropes beside it; new oars waited for the rowers; and a strong anchor, its rope neatly coiled, lay on the deck at the bow. Could any human being do so much in so little time? No, this must be the work of a god.

Soon the crew arrived. "Come to the palace with me," Telemachus told his men. "We must collect our supplies. Be careful, we don't want to be seen."

Telemachus led the way, and the others followed him. It was bright-eyed Athene who had disguised herself as Mentor. Now the goddess threw a mist over Telemachus and his men, so that nobody saw them enter or leave the palace. They carried the flagons of wine, the leather bags of ground barley and the other supplies to the ship. It was easy. Heavy burdens are light when a god is helping. They boarded. The goddess, still disguised as Mentor, took a seat near the stern, Telemachus beside her. The sailors cast off, then jumped aboard and took the oars. Athene called up a helping wind. "Hoist the sail," cried Telemachus, and soon the white sail bellied out with the good wind, and the ship flew over the choppy sea.

At the palace in Ithaca, the singer told about the birth of the goddess Athene. Athene was her father's child, and her father was Zeus, king of the immortals. Before her birth, Zeus had the biggest headache of all time, and no wonder. Finally, Hermes fetched an axe to split the god-king's forehead, and Zeus's daughter Athene, grown-up and armed with a round shield and a sharp spear, leaped out! Penelope stood listening by a pillar in the great hall. She smiled as if she had nothing on her mind but the song.

"How can you be so happy?" asked Kleea.

"It's not hard to look happy." Penelope spoke softly, hiding her mouth behind her hand. "Let them watch and see me behaving the way I always do. They won't miss Telemachus. Even if someone notices that he isn't here, they won't think it's important." When the queen went to bed at last, however, she did not expect to sleep. Athene closed her eyes and sent good dreams. In her sleep, the mother watched her son's ship fly over the water while twenty good men bent over their heavy oars.

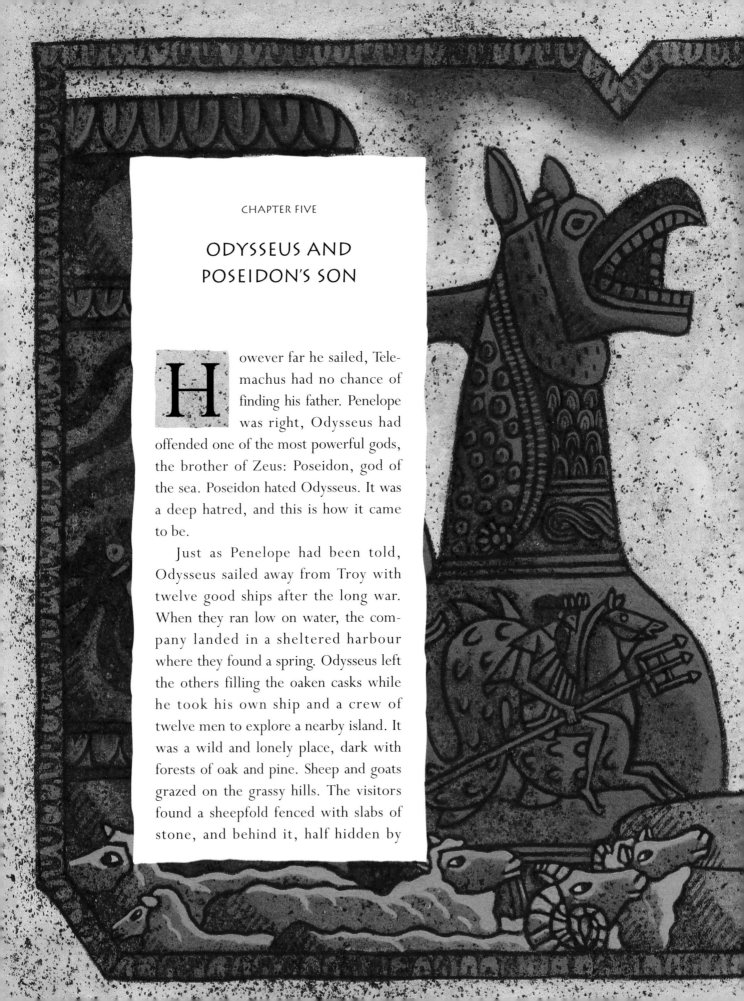

CHAPTER FIVE

ODYSSEUS AND POSEIDON'S SON

However far he sailed, Telemachus had no chance of finding his father. Penelope was right, Odysseus had offended one of the most powerful gods, the brother of Zeus: Poseidon, god of the sea. Poseidon hated Odysseus. It was a deep hatred, and this is how it came to be.

Just as Penelope had been told, Odysseus sailed away from Troy with twelve good ships after the long war. When they ran low on water, the company landed in a sheltered harbour where they found a spring. Odysseus left the others filling the oaken casks while he took his own ship and a crew of twelve men to explore a nearby island. It was a wild and lonely place, dark with forests of oak and pine. Sheep and goats grazed on the grassy hills. The visitors found a sheepfold fenced with slabs of stone, and behind it, half hidden by

trees, framed by immense stones, the entrance to a cave. What creature might have built such a place? A wild man, Odysseus thought, a giant. Rich, certainly. Generous to his guests, probably. Odysseus was determined to meet him.

Odysseus was the first to enter the cave, but his men were not far behind. Inside was a treasure of grain, wine and oil, packed in gigantic jars and sacks, not one of which was small enough for a strong man to lift. Huge cheeses lined one wall. Vats the size of bathtubs lay full of milk and cream. Odysseus's crew wanted to steal as much as they could carry and get away quickly. "We're sure a monster lives here," they told him.

"A giant, likely," Odysseus agreed. "His presents will be as big as he is. Think how happy our wives will be! You're not afraid, are you?" His men would not admit they were scared. Unluckily for them, as it turned out, they all waited for the owner of the cave to come back. Meanwhile, they ate a big meal, filling up on the giant's bread and cheese, washed down with the giant's milk and wine. Then they settled themselves in the inner part of the cave, not far from the fireplace, and fell asleep.

At sunset, a great shadow darkened the doorway. The caveman was indeed a giant, and a very ugly one at that, with only one huge glaring eye in the middle of his forehead! Odysseus knew this was a Cyclops, a very dangerous monster. He shepherded his flock into the cave and began to milk the ewes. He did not take all the milk from each, but left some for the lambs. As he finished milking each ewe, he put her lamb beside her, talking gently to the animals as he worked. Then he lifted a rock and set it in the entrance, so that the entrance was totally blocked. The giant did this easily, but Odysseus and his men could see that they could not possibly move the rock: it was far too big and heavy for that!

Now the giant came to the back of the cave and built up his fire, using whole trees for kindling. As the fire blazed up, he saw Odysseus and his men. "Visitors," he boomed. "I knew somebody had been here. What have you been stealing?"

"We helped ourselves to some of your good food, like hungry travellers," protested Odysseus. "You have plenty, we were sure you'd be happy to share it."

"Happy, of course," replied the giant, with an evil smile. "Fair's fair. I've given you your dinner. Now you can give me mine." With that he picked up two of the men, one in each enormous hand, and dashed their brains out on the floor. While Odysseus and the others looked on in horror, the giant tore the bodies apart and ate every bit, crunching the bones in his big white teeth. Then he lay down and went to sleep.

Odysseus drew his sword. Stepping softly, he went to the giant's head. Just as he was about to plunge the sharp point into the giant's neck, he saw his problem. He could kill the giant, but then he and his men would die in the cave. They could not move the stone away from the entrance. They could never escape.

"Why don't you kill him?" one of his men whispered angrily.

Odysseus looked at the great stone in the doorway. He made a motion of pushing, then shook his head. "Do you want to die in this cave?" he asked.

"We're going to die anyway," came the reply. "We should have run away when we had the chance."

"You should have listened to us," whined another man.

"We won't be taking any treasure home," groaned another. "We'll never see our families again."

"We're not dead yet," replied Odysseus. "Telemachus was a baby when I left Ithaca. Now he's half grown, if he's still alive. I intend to find out. I think of Penelope every day, just as you think of your families. I think of Ithaca and long to be home again. Keep up your courage, men. Think of home and getting there, and don't give up. I'm not going to be a monster's dinner."

The next morning, the giant ate two more of his guests for breakfast. "You are welcome to have some more of my bread and cheese," he chuckled as he left the cave. He moved the doorstone to get out, but put it back immediately.

Odysseus looked around the cave, his mind furiously at work. He had brought his men into this danger; how could he get them out? Rather, how could he trick the giant into setting all of them free? His eye fell on a fresh-cut log of olive wood. "I've got it," he exclaimed. He beckoned to three of his men. "Help me scrape the bark off this log and sharpen the end," he told them. "This will be our weapon. We'll draw lots to see who will help me use it."

At sunset the giant returned with his sheep. Again he milked his ewes. Again he killed and ate two of Odysseus's men. Now Odysseus had his chance. For a gift, he had brought rare wine, smooth as honey, sweet and very strong. Usually, one cup of the liquor would be mixed with twenty cups of water. Now Odysseus poured the heady wine into a wooden bowl and brought it to the monster. "Here, Cyclops," he coaxed, "have some wine to wash down that meal of human flesh!"

The giant gulped down the ruby liquid, fiery and smooth in his throat. "I've never tasted better," he exclaimed. "Give me some more. And tell me your name, so that I can give you something in exchange."

"My name is Nobody," said Odysseus.

"Nobody, is it," replied the giant. "All right, Nobody, here's your present: I'll eat all the others first. I'll save you to the last." He was still laughing at his own joke when he finished the third bowl of Odysseus's liquor and toppled to the floor, where he lay in a drunken stupor with his neck twisted to one side.

Odysseus built up the fire and heated the sharp tip of his wooden stake until the green wood almost caught fire. His men rammed this weapon into the giant's eye, while Odysseus hung on top, using his weight to drive it deep. A scream tore from the caveman's throat. He pulled the huge stake out of his eye, which streamed with blood. In agony, he cried out for help from his relatives who lived in caves not far away. They asked, "What's wrong, brother? Why are you making all this noise? Is somebody trying to kill you?"

The Cyclops answered, "Nobody's trying to kill me."

"Well then," the others told him, "if nobody's trying to kill you, but you're making all this noise, you must be sick. That kind of sickness comes from the gods. There's nothing we can do about it. You'd better pray to our father Poseidon to make you better."

If Odysseus had been listening carefully, he might have heard Poseidon's name. He was not listening, however. He was feeling very pleased with his own cleverness. Nobody! He couldn't have thought of a better name. The pleased feeling stayed with him as he tied the sheep together in groups of three. Underneath each group of three, he tied one of his men. "You may not get much sleep," he whispered to them, "but you're not going to be eaten for breakfast." Then he slung himself underneath the belly of the great ram, the leader of the flock, gripping the tangled wool with his hands

and knees. It would not be easy to hang on, but Odysseus never thought of getting himself tied under a group of sheep and leaving one of his men to take the most dangerous place.

When morning came, the Cyclops rolled away the doorstone to let his animals out to graze. With his great hands, he felt the backs of the sheep to make sure none of the men was getting away, but he did not feel underneath their bellies. The ram, slowed down by Odysseus's weight, was last to leave the cave. "Old friend," said the Cyclops, "you're sorry for me, aren't you. You always lead the others outside in the morning, but today you have stayed behind." He patted the animal's great head. Odysseus was going numb from the strain. If the ram did not get out soon, he was sure to fall. "Get along with you," said the Cyclops fondly, and the ram struggled out into the sunlight.

Odysseus was shaking with the strain when he let go of the creature and rolled out from underneath it. He untied his men, and they hurried down to their ship. They were all somewhat surprised to be alive and free. The breeze stirred their hair. The sun warmed them. One of them started to laugh, and all the others joined in. For the moment, they forgot about their six comrades and the horror of their deaths.

"Let's go." Odysseus nodded toward the ship. Quickly, they rowed out to sea, but Odysseus couldn't just slip away: he had to show how clever he had been. "Cyclops," he called, "you got what you deserved for eating your guests."

The giant had lost his eye, but not his ears. He picked up a piece of the cliff and threw it toward the sound of Odysseus's voice. His aim was very good. The vast rock fell just beyond the bow of the ship; pushed by the waves, the ship flew back to shore.

Odysseus grabbed a boathook and pushed off again. "Row, row," he urged, but his men were already in a racing stroke. Now he waited until the ship was twice as far from land before he taunted the giant once more.

"Cyclops," he screamed, "I want you to know who blinded you. I'm not Nobody, I'm Odysseus, Sacker of Cities, son of Laertes, who lives in Ithaca."

The Cyclops gave a groan. "I knew it," he roared. "Years ago a prophet told me Odysseus would steal my sight. I always thought he'd be another giant, not a puny little thing like you." Now the Cyclops called on Poseidon, the great god of the sea, brother of Zeus. "Hear me, Poseidon," he cried. "If I really am your son, then use your power to punish this Odysseus who has blinded me. Don't let him get home to Ithaca. If that is beyond even your power, let him wander for long, long years, let all his ships be sunk and his companions killed, and let everything go badly in his home."

The giant threw another huge boulder, but the men had kept rowing madly and the missile fell just short of the steering oar. This time the waves drove the ship on toward the harbour where their comrades waited. Odysseus got away, but at great cost. He could never get home without crossing the water, where Poseidon ruled. From this time on, the ocean was his enemy.

CHAPTER SIX

AUTUMN
AT THE FARM

Penelope did not know about the Cyclops or about the sea-god's hatred for her husband. She did not know anything that had happened after he started home from Troy. Now that the suitors knew how she had tricked them, she went on working every day at her loom, but she no longer came down to undo the work at night. Scenes from Laertes' life took form as she wove. Every day she wound more finished cloth onto the roll at the top. One or another of the suitors watched every move.

Eurymachus was the watcher one day. "Such exquisite weaving, Queen Penelope," he remarked. "The leaves are finished, aren't they. Are you starting a hunting scene?" He leaned over the queen's shoulder. "I like to watch the shuttle in your white hands. You're so sure of yourself. What a pity I did not stand beside you long ago!"

Penelope stood still. "You're in my way," she warned. "You're welcome to get in my way, of course, if that is what you want to do."

Eurymachus stepped back quickly. "I would not want to slow you down," he sneered. "My friends and I appreciate your skill. We want to watch your work, but we certainly do not want to get in your way."

"You have never been interested in women's work before," replied Penelope. "I don't know why my weaving is so interesting to you now."

"You know very well." Eurymachus's face got red. He made a fist with his right hand and pounded it rhythmically against his left. He forgot about pretending to be polite. "You have worked at that weaving, doing and undoing, for three years already. Now finish it. We're watching. Finish it quickly, lady, the old king may need it very soon. In this world there are times for waiting and times for action. The time for waiting is over, Penelope. It's time you chose another husband. We have waited long enough."

Antinous nodded. His spy in town had told him about Telemachus. What a pity he'd gone to look for his father. Obviously, he was no longer a boy but a man, and dangerous. Probably they would have to kill Telemachus after all. He looked at Penelope. How sad she would be! Perhaps Telemachus would disappear and she would never know what had happened to him. That might be best. He would give her other sons.

Penelope forced herself to ignore the men. Quietly, she moved back and forth in front of the big loom.

Day by day, the web grew. Aleta was never far away. As much as she could, the girl watched the watchers. "They're taking turns," she told Penelope and Kleea.

"I'm not surprised," Penelope nodded.

Soon Aleta had more bad news. "Everybody knows about Telemachus," she told them. "The men are really angry. I can't hear much these days, they don't trust me, but that much is easy to see."

"Be careful," urged Penelope. "You've done well. We don't want you getting hurt, do we." She smiled at Kleea.

"I get angry at myself." Kleea's voice shook with frustration. "My bones are stiff. I can't hide under tables or crouch in a corner, not any more. It's hard to get down on my knees and harder to get up again. I'd give my life for you, my Queen, and I'm useless."

"That's not true." Penelope was calm. "You help as you always have. You run the household. You can't spy on the suitors, but you watch the women all the time and listen to them. You know who's loyal and who's not, and you tell me, so I know too. I talk to you in ways I don't to anyone else. When I cannot stop crying, you hold me in your arms. You bathe me, you brush my hair. Don't forget how important you are. I may not remind you very often." Penelope's hand rested fondly on Kleea's arm. Both women were silent for a long time. Aleta felt full of pride.

At last Penelope spoke again. "Today, I need your wisdom, Kleea. My weaving is almost finished. What are we going to do?"

"I don't know what to suggest." Kleea was exasperated. "Every time I turn around, something else makes me angry. I can't get away from those bullies downstairs and our people who are working with them. Even here in your own room, I can hear them laughing. I can smell the blood of our slaughtered swine and sheep."

The inspiration was Aleta's, although Penelope and Kleea wondered why the idea had not occurred to either of them. "I wish we could go to the farm and stay with Lord Laertes," Aleta said. "I remember how quiet and peaceful it was. How good the apples smelled! I could sleep in the hayloft again and feed the chickens and gather the eggs. Maybe I could learn to milk the goats, now that I'm older. Lord Laertes wouldn't mind. Can't we go to the farm?"

Penelope's eyes brightened. So did Kleea's. "Yes, indeed," replied the queen. She clapped her hands. "Why didn't I think of it myself? The air here stinks of slaughtered beasts and cooking fires. It's poisoned with treachery and fear. We'll get away for a few days. Safely too, Mentor sent word only yesterday. At present the roads are clear of robbers. It's time, and more than time, we paid a visit to the old king. Kleea, how soon can we be ready? Can we leave tomorrow?"

"I'm sure we can." Kleea was already making lists in her head: warm clothes, food, pack animals, an escort, gifts for the old king and his household. She clambered stiffly to her feet.

"We'll go early," Penelope commanded, "before the palace is stirring. Now what will I tell the suitors? I won't tell them that I've only got a few more days of weaving before the shroud comes off my loom." She thought for a moment. "How's this? I'll tell Antinous I've had a message from the old king and must go to him for a few days. I trust Antinous more than most of them, even though it may not be wise. We were born in the same land."

"He'll be flattered," Kleea replied. "Eurymachus won't be pleased, but you don't care about that!"

They slipped downstairs in the darkness just before dawn, passing like shadows through the great hall. Along the far wall men lay snoring, but nobody stirred. Perhaps Athene was once more holding them in sleep. Aleta felt as if she could walk all day, even though she had been up most of the night helping her grandmother. Outside the great door, they paused in the grey half-light. "Here's your warm cloak, Aleta, put it on," said Kleea softly. "The mules are loaded. The cowherd and his son are waiting. Only two men, that's a poor escort for a queen!" She shook her head.

"Two good men whom I trust, and no spies," replied Penelope. She led Kleea and Aleta toward the courtyard gate, talking as she went. "We don't look like a royal party. If the gods will it, we'll go and come back safely. It's only for five days," she added. "I won't stay away longer than that. But we'll have some time to think and talk as we go, as well as when we're there. I feel better already. We'll talk to dear old Laertes. Maybe he can help."

"Don't get too hopeful," Kleea advised. She frowned. "It's hard for me to say that. King Laertes brought me here when he married, and paid my father a great price, too. I loved him then, and I love him still. I owe him a debt that couldn't be paid with gold." She looked sideways at Aleta. "But the heart went out of him long ago. He's tired right through to his bones. He takes what life hands him, he doesn't struggle any more."

"I expect you're right," Penelope admitted, "though I think he'd be different if Odysseus came home. Well, we'll have time and space, and that will be a blessing. Do you think Antinous believed me, Kleea, about the message?"

"Maybe, maybe not," Kleea shrugged. "Does it matter? It seems like old times, going to the farm." Now Kleea moved briskly. She seemed at least ten years younger. Aleta ran to open the courtyard gate.

Two men stood outside it. She knew the older man, the cowherd, she'd seen him often with animals to be killed for the suitors to eat. His son was patting a mule's nose. A second mule stood behind him, nuzzling his shoulder. Both animals were loaded. Aleta looked again and smiled, recognizing the bags she and Kleea had packed the night before. The cowman held the bridle of a third mule, saddled for riding. He touched his forehead in respect, but he did not bow his head. He had served Penelope since her marriage. He and the queen were not strangers. "Will you ride, lady?" he asked. She nodded, and he made a step with his hands so she could mount. She waved him forward and the little cavalcade set forth, the older man in front, followed by Penelope, and the younger one, with the pack beasts, a little distance behind Kleea and her granddaughter.

Ithaca is an island of rocky hills. No path there is easy for those on foot. However, all that party were on holiday. The oak leaves had turned dark

yellow and brown. Some still clung to the trees, but the travellers scuffled happily through others that had been blown down by the autumn winds. Despite the chill, it was a glorious morning. The sun shone golden in a cloudless deep blue sky. "Phoebus Apollo is good to us today," laughed Penelope. "When you were a child, Kleea, did you pretend you could see the great god driving the chariot of the sun across the sky?"

"Of course," Kleea replied. "Doesn't every child? My mother cured me of looking, though. She wasn't going to let me be blinded by the god." She patted Aleta's shoulder.

"My grandmother cured me," said Aleta boldly. She remembered the beating very well. It was the only one her grandmother had ever given her.

"You've always been a good child." Kleea's voice was warm.

Soon the track began to climb, gently at first, then steep and twisting into the hills. Penelope rode for the first hour or so, but soon she was on her feet, striding cheerfully along the path. "Your turn, Kleea," she insisted, laughing off the old woman's protest. "The soil of Ithaca feels good under my feet."

Aleta skipped along beside the cowherd, chattering happily about the days when her mother served Lord Laertes and they both lived at the farm. The man already knew the story of the fire, there'd been enough gossip about it at the time, but he didn't say so. Why put a cloud in the girl's bright sky? If she had forgotten about it, and it seemed as if she had, he wouldn't be the one to remind her.

They stopped briefly at noon by a spring and ate their meal of bread and goat's cheese, washed down with water. Then they went on, uphill and down. Birds sang. A vulture wheeled lazily overhead for a while and then disappeared. Once the cowherd stopped and pointed. Aleta, following his finger, glimpsed a deer. She felt as if she could go on walking like this forever. Nobody seemed the least bit tired, although the sun was getting low and they had all wrapped their cloaks closely around their bodies by the time the cowherd made the announcement, "There it is."

They moved a little faster to the top of the hill where he was standing, and there it was, not far away, a small, low house in the middle of a scattering of barns and sheds. Their path now led them by vines that were heavy with purple grapes.

"Give me those mules," the cowherd told his son. He held out his hand for the bridles. "Run ahead and tell them we're almost here."

"It's smaller," said Aleta slowly. She sounded puzzled.

"What is, the house?" asked the cowherd.

Kleea broke in, "It's been a long time since you were here, Aleta. You're much bigger now."

When the queen arrived, King Laertes stood at the door. "Greetings, Penelope, wife of my dear son Odysseus," he saluted her. "What fortune brings you here? I hope it's good fortune, but so many bad things have happened, I'm afraid this is more bad news. Are those wicked suitors still making trouble? But I'm forgetting my manners. Come in. Here I am asking you questions, and you must be tired." The old man beckoned to his servant, a wrinkled crone who had lived on the farm all her life. "Wash the queen's feet," he commanded, "and bring wine and meat for everybody. After you've rested, Penelope, we can talk. Kleea, it's good to see you, and Aleta, well! You were a baby when you left us, just a little girl, a little monkey, getting into everything. I missed you. And now you're a young lady. How old? Ten? Eleven years old?"

"I'm twelve years old." Aleta beamed. Her birthday had been a disappointment, with Telemachus gone. Nobody had made much of it. She hadn't been in the mood to celebrate it any more than the rest of them.

Laertes smiled at her. "We'll drink a toast to twelve years old," he said. "Kleea, make sure I don't forget."

"Thanks, dear Father," smiled Penelope. He was her husband's father, of course, not hers, but that didn't make any difference to how they felt about each other. "You always think of others, and make them comfortable. That's one reason I love you." Laertes put his arm around her shoulder, and everybody went inside. "I told the suitors I had a message that you were ill," Penelope continued. "But really, Laertes, it was a good thing I came. You're not looking after yourself the way you should, that's obvious." She laughed fondly at the old man.

Laertes looked down at his clothes. His tunic was patched and filthy. He wore a battered old pair of leather shin protectors. Old gardening gloves and a goatskin hat lay on a table where he had dropped them. "I spend my days in the garden. These are gardeners' clothes." He shrugged. "It's better than hanging around that palace of yours, listening to the suitors insult you."

The old woman brought wine and golden apples, but nothing else. "Where is the rest of the meal?" Laertes asked.

"I don't know what to do," she answered. "I've made a lentil stew. There's plenty of it, but how can I think of serving stew to the queen?"

Penelope burst out laughing, and after a moment or two everybody joined in. "I smelled it the minute we stepped inside," she said. "If the taste is as good as the smell, I'll be well satisfied." The cowherd built up the fire. They sat on plain stools, not carved chairs, and ate their stew and coarse bread at a table of planks. Penelope spoke for all of them, however, when she told Laertes, "This is the best meal I've had in years."

Aleta nodded off to sleep before they were done eating. The cowherd caught her just as she began to fall. She didn't stir when he carried her up the ladder to the loft and laid her gently on her bed of straw. The others went to sleep not much later.

"Your hair's all tangles tonight," grumbled Kleea, hairbrush in hand.

Penelope nodded. "It can wait till morning," she said. "Everything can wait till morning. You're right about Laertes, I'm afraid. He won't be much help."

"Ask him anyway," urged Kleea. "No harm in asking."

"No," replied Laertes next morning. "I would love to throw those lazy good-for-nothings out of the palace. They're eating my crops and drinking my wine." He flexed his fingers longingly. "But there's nothing I can do, much though I hate to admit it. Besides, this is harvest time, Penelope. I'm surprised you didn't think of that. Dolius and his six sons have been in the fields since dawn. Today we're cutting wheat. Tomorrow we start the millet. We have twelve different kinds of grapes. Had you forgotten? We've been harvesting grapes for a month already, and we'll be picking until they freeze. The wine will be good this year." His head was bowed. He lifted it and looked at her. "I'd leave it all and come with you if I could help," he said. "Maybe I should come with you anyway."

"No." Penelope took his arm. She smiled at him as they walked together. He is a wonderful old man, she thought, but he's just too old. "You look after the farm. We'll manage. Telemachus is sure that one of the great gods is helping us," she added. "He knows he'll get news of his father." Penelope tried to sound as confident as Telemachus had been. With Laertes she walked round the orchard. "I hate to see your beautiful apples and pears go to feed those thieves back at the palace," she fumed. "I hate them to drink the wine you make. But it can't be helped. I may have to marry one of them before long."

"If you have to do that, I'll understand," replied Laertes.

As they turned back, they could see two female figures running toward them. Aleta was easy to recognize, but who was with her? "Nesta?" queried Penelope. "What's she doing here?"

Laertes snorted. "I've forgotten many things," he said, "but I'll never forget Nesta, not to my dying day. Not till I drink the water of Lethe in the afterworld. I did not think she'd show her face here. Aleta hasn't said a word."

"She's forgotten about the fire, I think," replied Penelope. "Sometimes the gods help us to forget things too terrible to remember."

"Yes," added Laertes, "and she was very young. We hoped she would forget, didn't we. It was the right decision, moving her and Nesta to the palace."

"It was the best thing we could think of," Penelope agreed, "though Nesta hasn't ever been much help. Poor Kleea! But Aleta more than makes up for her mother. She's acting like a child here, and I'm glad of it. At the palace, she's had to learn to act far older than her years. I didn't realize how much it weighs on me. We all do what we must." She sighed, watching Aleta and her mother approach. "I'm sure Nesta does not bring good news."

Laertes reached up to pick a winter pear and handed it to Penelope. Her fingers caressed its red-gold skin. "I won't stay," the old man said abruptly. "I'm going back to the house." He turned and strode off as Nesta and Aleta came up. Aleta was crying quietly.

"Well, Nesta?" asked Penelope. "What brings you here?"

Aleta and her mother began talking at the same time. "It's terrible," Aleta gulped. She stopped. This was Nesta's story.

"Some of the suitors got hold of a ship," panted Nesta. "They're hiding in an island cove. Telemachus will come back that way, and they'll attack. They'll kill everybody and sink the ship." She stopped for breath. "They're sure they won't be caught. Pirates will be blamed, or a deadly storm." She shivered. "Telemachus will never come home, but nobody will know exactly how he died."

"I suppose your friends are in the plot." Penelope frowned. Nesta shrugged helplessly but did not reply. After a moment Penelope went on, "Nesta, why did you come here to tell me about it? Lord Laertes is very angry at you." Penelope felt cold, although the afternoon sun still held some warmth.

"Didn't you want to know about it?" Nesta asked. "I was worried about Aleta, as close to you as she is, and I'm a coward, you know that." She paused for a long time, then went on in a very low voice. "I loved

Telemachus when he was a baby. When Mother was angry with me, I would rock him sometimes and pretend he was my little brother. I don't want him to die."

"I didn't know that, Nesta," Penelope gently replied. "Thank you. You're less of a coward than either of us thought."

Nesta shrugged. "It was safer to come here, where I know the wrong people can't hear us. Lord Laertes needn't worry, I'm not staying. You believe me?" she asked.

"Oh, I believe you, it's just like them, cowards, bullies, killers. I wish I thought you were lying." Penelope's face was very pale.

Aleta put her arms around the queen and hugged her. She would never have dared to do this at home, but everything was different at the farm. Penelope was not dressed like a queen; she wore an old tunic over a simple woollen skirt. Aleta's head nestled against her chest. She could feel the queen's heart beating. Penelope held her close. "There's no standing still," she said, speaking over Aleta's shoulder to Nesta. "That's not possible. My weaving is almost done. I'll summon those murderous brutes and keep them busy at the palace. I'll tell them I'm going to choose a husband."

"They'll come back in a hurry," Nesta declared. "I don't think they'll forget their plan, all the same. They'll try to kill Telemachus some other way. I've told you, though, that's all I can do. I'll go back now. I know this countryside, and there is a moon. I can run through the night. Goodbye, Aleta. Stay well, child." She turned and was gone.

"Why didn't Mother stay?" asked Aleta. "I'm sure she was tired and hungry, and she was trying to help. Lord Laertes used to like her, didn't he? What happened all those years ago? Why is the old king so angry at my mother?"

Penelope shook her head, but did not answer. She took Aleta's hand, and they walked together down the hill. Now Aleta's head was full of the old questions. She had thought of them often, in one form or another, though not for a long time: Why do I stay with Grandmother and not with Mother, though we live in the same house? Grandmother has been ashamed of her daughter ever since I can remember. Why has it always been like this?

Aleta slept again on her bed of straw. She dreamed of fire, of flames bursting through the wall, leaping toward her. Scream, scream for help, commanded her nightmare mind, but a fist held her throat so that she could not scream. She woke suddenly and was on her feet, crouched to run, before she realized that there was no smoke or flame. The loft was dark.

CHAPTER SEVEN

PENELOPE ANNOUNCES A CONTEST

N esta ran through the night. She remembered the road well enough, and the full moon guided her. All the same, she knew she could easily twist a foot or break an ankle. Every rabbit hole, every stone and shadow was a danger. She stopped twice for food and water, and once to relieve herself. Each time, it was harder to go on again. When at last she saw the dark mass of the palace, she was exhausted from anxiety as well as from the run. The great door was bolted, as she knew it would be, but the little door was open. Nesta slipped inside and curled up thankfully on the hard-packed floor.

"Wake up, Nesta. Why are you sleeping here?" Fingers poked her arm. Nesta opened blurry eyes. "It's about time," hissed sharp-faced Helen. "What's wrong with you? The men want their laundry done, and I said we'd do it. Then we'll

have a picnic. Get up, lazybones. The queen will come back soon. This may be our last day of freedom. For a while." Helen laughed softly.

Castor and Eurymachus had piled up rich tunics and heavy woollen cloaks. "I think they've given us all the clothes they own," grumbled Helen. Nesta did not reply. They packed the clothes into a great basket and lugged it down to the river, to the washing pools. They tied up their long skirts. Then they started to throw the dirty clothes into the river and trample out the dirt. The water was knee-deep and icy cold. Soon the fog of tiredness cleared from Nesta's head. Before long, she and Helen were flicking water at each other and giggling. They hauled out the clothes and spread them on the rocky shore. They dried each other and brushed each other's hair.

"The men won't be here for a while," said Helen suddenly. "What have you been up to, Nesta? I want to know."

"What?" Nesta gaped. Why had she hoped that Helen would stop her questions?

"You know what," snapped Helen. "Where were you yesterday and all last night? You've been doing something you don't want me to know about, I can see it in your face." Her eyes narrowed. "You wouldn't try to warn them, would you, about Telemachus?"

"No, no." Nesta was shocked. How could anybody keep a secret from Helen? She could play and laugh as if she wasn't thinking about anything. You thought you were safe, and all the time she was sharpening her claws. Like a cat with a mouse. But Nesta was determined not to let Helen know about her visit to the farm. She thought about Telemachus instead. "I'm sorry for him," she said. "He's just a boy. What can he do against a hundred men? There's no need to murder him."

"Don't change the subject, Nesta. What were you doing? Did you think I wouldn't notice?"

"I don't know what you're talking about," blurted Nesta. "I told you what I was doing. I told you yesterday. I was sick. I went to Hera's shrine."

"Hera, indeed," sneered Helen. "Are you having another baby, is that it? Hera would want you to have a husband first."

Tears gathered in Nesta's eyes. Sometimes she was glad she cried so easily. "I thought you were my friend," she sobbed.

"I am your friend," Helen told her, "you know I am. We've been friends forever. Sometimes you make me furious, all the same. Don't be so weak, Nesta. Were you really at Hera's shrine?" Nesta, still crying, nodded. Helen patted her shoulder. "All right," she soothed, "you were at Hera's shrine. Did the goddess speak to you?" Nesta shook her head. "Stop your snivelling," ordered Helen, but the sting had gone out of her voice. "I won't bite you. Go and wash your face, silly, the men will be here any minute. Don't go sneaking off again, will you. It puts nasty ideas into my head."

Castor and Eurymachus brought a hamper of food and a goatskin full of wine. After lunch Castor brought out a ball and they played catch.

"The clothes will be dry by now," said Helen at last. "Start packing, Nesta. I'll come and help you in a minute or two." Nesta got the basket and started to work. Helen watched while she talked to Eurymachus and Castor. When Nesta looked up, Helen smiled at her and waved. "Nesta has changed," Helen muttered. "She's up to something, and she's not telling us."

"You should know," Eurymachus nodded. "Have you noticed anything, Castor?"

"She loves me," Castor argued. "She'll do anything for me. Who stole the storeroom key? Nesta did. She hasn't changed."

"That was months ago," replied Helen. "I tell you, I've been watching her. Something isn't right. I think she's watching me too."

"Maybe that's all it is," said Eurymachus thoughtfully. "She sees you watching her. She wonders why. She watches you."

"It doesn't feel like that." Helen shook her head.

"You're a sharp woman." Eurymachus put his arm around her. He would never say so, but sometimes Helen was too sharp for comfort.

He was not sure he would take her home with him. Meantime, Helen was very useful; he'd keep on her good side. "Nesta doesn't help us much these days. She knows too much, if we're not sure of her. Why take a chance?" As he spoke, Eurymachus looked thoughtfully down at the rocks and the river pools beyond. "This is a good place for an accident," he mused. "A woman could easily slip on the rocks, bang her head and fall into the water." He looked down at his big hands.

Castor was shocked. "No!" he blurted. "You and your feelings, Helen. You're not sure of anything. Nesta is one of us." Castor liked Nesta to sit on his knee and drink with him. He liked her to curl up with him at night. He hadn't seen much of her lately, all the same. That would have to change.

"We'll wait," soothed Eurymachus. He did not want a fight with Castor. "I hope you're right about her." Helen nodded. She did not want Nesta to be killed for no good reason. "Watch her, both of you," ordered Eurymachus. "Report to me every day. Off you go now, Helen, before she packs up all the clothes."

∾∾∾∾

Penelope and her party reached the palace only a short time after the four picnickers got back. Kleea, exhausted, went straight to bed.

"You too, Aleta," Penelope ordered. "You must be tired too. I'll go downstairs as usual."

"I'm not tired," Aleta insisted. "Let me bathe your feet and help you dress. Let me fix your hair."

"Brave girl!" replied Penelope. "I want to look my best. I have something important to say to the suitors."

Aleta took down the cascades of black hair, so long that Penelope could easily sit on it. It was tangled after another day in the open, and she worked over it, pulling the knots apart. She brushed the wings at Penelope's temples. "Tell me if I'm hurting you, my lady," she said.

"You're a good help to your grandmother," Penelope reflected. "And to me. You aren't hurting me, child, I'm thinking. It's worse here since we went away. I can feel wickedness in the air."

Aleta shivered. "I can feel it too," she agreed. Why did she think of her mother as she spoke? She steadied the hand that held the hairbrush. "Maybe Telemachus is right, and a god is helping us. Then we'll be all right."

"Unless a stronger god is helping the others," said Penelope. "Provided we don't do something that makes our god angry. Gods seldom do what people expect." She shook her head, as if to shake such thoughts away. "Athene has always been a friend to Odysseus and his family. Few gods are more powerful than she is. Come, Aleta, let's go down."

That evening, the party seemed quieter than usual. At first Aleta was pleased, but then she remembered the message her mother had brought. Some of the suitors were on a ship waiting to murder Telemachus and all his crew. No wonder there was less noise in the hall. Penelope stood beside a pillar near the back, Aleta by her side. Men and women rushed about filling the suitors' plates and cups, the men carrying great platters of roast meat and the women bearing flagons of mellow wine or baskets with loaves of fresh bread. Aleta tugged at the queen's hand. Penelope's eyes followed where the girl pointed. She saw the empty places. Eurymachus stood up and came over to them. "Have some of my suitors gone home?" Penelope asked. "Am I not to have their company any longer?"

"Who would give up hope of marrying you?" replied Eurymachus smoothly. "A few of your faithful suitors went away when you did. The palace was dull without you. They will be glad to hear that you noticed."

Penelope's eyes blazed, but she bit back her angry reply. She knew what her "faithful suitors" were doing, the murderous thugs: they were lying in wait for Telemachus. It was hard to speak politely, but Penelope had had a lot of practice in hiding her true feelings. Now she was fighting for the life of her son. "You have been so patient," she told Eurymachus. "I've kept you waiting for a long time. Now even I am not sure that my husband will ever come back."

Eurymachus bowed. "We knew it," he agreed. "After so many years, Odysseus will not return. I'm glad to hear you say it. Does this mean you are ready to choose your new husband?" His eyes gleamed.

"Soon," replied Penelope steadily. Never, if I can help it, she thought. "My weaving is almost finished. It's an important decision, choosing a husband. I can't think about it seriously until everybody is here. I want to see all of you every day. It's not that I don't know all of you, after such a long time, but I have not been thinking about marrying one of you. I'm bound to see you differently, thinking of that. I'll ask you to give me presents, and they should be good ones. You've been eating and drinking here for such a long time, that's only fair. Telemachus can forget about being king. My new husband will rule in Ithaca."

At last, thought Eurymachus. His lips curved happily.

"Why should I choose one of you rather than another?" the queen continued. "You'll have to tell me. Why should I choose you, Eurymachus, and not Castor?" Penelope turned to look at Castor. "Or why, Castor, should you be the lucky one? Perhaps I'll decide on an athletic competition. Who can run fastest? Who is best with a javelin, or bow and arrow? But we won't begin until everybody is here. The men who are away would be angry. They would say I'm not being fair to them. Don't you agree?"

"What are you really thinking, Queen Penelope?" Eurymachus found himself remembering how Penelope had made a fool of him with her weaving. "You've never talked like this before."

Penelope smiled, not pleasantly. "I like the idea of a contest," she said, and was surprised to find the words were true. For a moment she had forgotten that these men were trying to kill her son. The smile froze on her lips. She wanted to hurl her words like javelins: Murderers! Cowards! I want you here where I can see you, all of you. While you are eating and drinking, my family is getting poor, but Telemachus is safe.

Penelope did not hurl the javelin words. She took a deep breath. Another. At last she spoke. "This is my promise. Eurymachus, two weeks after all of you have brought your gifts, I will choose a husband." Penelope could feel herself trembling. She pulled up her scarf to hide her face, then turned to go upstairs to her room. Aleta ran ahead to open the door.

The queen was pleased she'd be sleeping in her own bed again, the great bed that Odysseus had carved when they were married. Aleta unpinned her hair quickly and took up the brush, but Penelope shook her head. "No more tonight, Aleta, thank you. I hope we're not too tired to sleep. Make your bed by the door, I'd like you close at hand."

Later, Athene of the flashing eyes looked down at the queen. The warrior goddess herself bent to close Penelope's tired eyes. If the sleepers could have seen her, they would have seen a radiant smile. "I put the idea of this contest in your head, my wise Penelope," they would have heard her say. "Your plan will bring the rest of the suitors back here quickly. They won't wait to kill Telemachus. I'll send his ship a different way, all the same. Now sleep, and dream of your husband, Penelope, perhaps he will come home."

In the queen's dream, a boat landed on a lonely beach. The sleeper could not tell the place, but she knew it was somewhere in Ithaca. Men pulled the boat up on the sand. They lifted out something long and heavy, rolled in a blanket. They carried their burden up the beach, well past where the tide might rise, and gently laid it down. Was it a body? Beside the still form, the sailors heaped up treasure: a wooden strongbox full of rich clothing and gold ornaments, and beside it tripods and cauldrons of bronze, inlaid with rich designs.

Was he alive? The dreamer could not tell. Mist rolled in and hid the scene. Penelope smiled in her sleep and held her arms to her body, as if she were holding the husband she had waited for so long.

CHAPTER EIGHT

TELEMACHUS RETURNS

Aleta and Nesta passed each other in the hall or in the women's quarters more than once each day. "Stop and talk to me," Aleta begged, but Nesta always shook her head and hurried on. Aleta could not forget the farm. How suddenly her mother had appeared, how quickly she had left! Lord Laertes refused to meet her.

What did you do, Mother? What happened long ago at the farm? Aleta longed to ask. She longed in vain. Her mother would not speak to her. The queen did not want to tell the story. She could not ask her grandmother. What could she do?

The answer came suddenly. I'll ask the goddess! Ask Athene. I'm not an important person, but I'm not asking for a big thing. Maybe she will help me.

How could Aleta get away? What sacrifice could she offer? She had nothing. At last she asked Kleea for help. "I want

to make a sacrifice for Telemachus to get back safely," she explained. "I'd like to go to Athene's shrine by myself."

"Good idea," replied Kleea. "Take some ripe olives and some olive oil. I know you feel close to Telemachus. Go this afternoon, if you like."

The shrine was surrounded by olive trees. The olive had been Athene's gift to mortals. Aleta was pleased to think that now she would give olives and olive oil back to the goddess.

I wasn't really lying to Grandmother, Aleta told herself as she walked along the lonely path. I will make a sacrifice for Telemachus as well as for myself. But what? She stooped and picked up a branch that had fallen in the path. An olive branch. If there were live coals at the shrine, she would burn it as her sacrifice.

When she knelt in front of the marble basin with her offerings, Aleta knew she had to begin with Telemachus. She could not come to the goddess for herself while she was deceiving her grandmother. That wasn't right. She put the olives in the basin and poured the oil on the ground. "Mighty Athene, protect Telemachus and help him to get home safe." The words were whispered, but she meant them with all her heart. She stayed on her knees for a long time, thinking about Telemachus.

Finally Aleta got up and went over to a little iron brazier. Would there be fire? She looked for dry leaves and a few small twigs before she lifted the clump of moss that covered the embers. A spark would be enough, she could coax it. She blew on the coals. At first, the fire seemed dead, then she saw a spark. She put a leaf beside it. The shrine was open to the sky, but a wall protected the brazier from wind. She blew again, then added leaves and twigs, and finally the olive branch. It caught and began to burn. "Thank you, goddess," Aleta breathed. "You have given me fire to make my offering."

The flame rose clear and bright. Aleta devoured it with her eyes. Everything vanished from her mind except her mother, her feelings, her questions. Suddenly the nightmare was there again, fire reaching for her, but this time she was awake, not asleep in bed. Aleta screamed and screamed, but the pictures did not stop. She felt the heat. She was a tiny child, helpless in her terror. She could not move. A spark landed on her face. In a moment she would blaze up and be gone.

Strong arms grabbed her. "Hang onto me," ordered King Laertes. "Don't let go." Aleta's fingers clenched, gripping her own cloak. She relived the scene, herself as a little child held against the king's goatskin vest, his gardening vest. Now she remembered precisely what had happened. The house blazed in the darkness, flames reaching for the sky. Then it was ashes, with black, ragged posts where the door had been. A foul stench filled her nostrils.

No wonder the farmhouse she had just visited had seemed small. "King Laertes had a much better house, before little Aleta burned it down." Whose voice was that?

And who replied, "But everyone was saved, the child too, thanks to Lord Laertes himself. They were burned, both of them, but nothing that wouldn't heal. A house can be built again."

Guilty memories flooded back, heavy on the thin, bent shoulders. Aleta knew exactly what she had done. It was as if she held the weighty poker again, pushed it into the smouldering fire on the hearth, laughed to see the flames blaze up, then watched helplessly as a burning log tumbled out onto her blanket and flame began to rise.

But finding one answer raised another question. Aleta puzzled over it. "King Laertes saved me. I burned his house down, and he was good to me, then and now. How could he stand to see me again? But he wouldn't see my mother. Why her? Why not me?"

As she thought the question, she heard her grandmother's bitter voice, as clear as if Kleea was standing there, "Always flighty, that Nesta, you can never count on her."

Aleta could guess why King Laertes blamed her mother and not herself. It was only a guess, but she was sure it must be right. Her mother had gone out. Three-year-old Aleta had been left alone. Not for the first time either, she was sure of that. In Aleta's vision, a crowd of people pointed at Nesta, faces red with anger, jeering. She could hear bits of what they were saying: "Leaving your child alone, just a baby, sneaking off with your friends, always looking for a party." "We've seen that baby full of cuts and bruises, it's a wonder she hasn't drowned or burned herself to death." "You're the guilty one!"

"I'd best take the child away." Kleea was talking to King Laertes. "She'll be better with me. I'd like it," she added. "She's a bright little thing, sunshine in my life."

"Take her mother too," Laertes said. "I've got a new house to build."

Kleea looked bitterly at her daughter.

What was her mother doing? Nesta stood sullen, silent, with her eyes on the ground. At last the scene faded from Aleta's mind.

At the shrine in the olive trees, the girl sobbed for a long time. At first, she wished she had never made her sacrifice. Then she was angry at the goddess. Why had Athene answered her prayers? Penelope was right, gods don't do what you expect. Knowledge has its price, and sometimes the price is high. Her new knowledge was important, however. Aleta knew now how much she owed to her grandmother and to the queen. She longed for someone to come and ask her to step in front of a knife or jump off a high cliff for Penelope or Kleea, but no one came. Athene's shrine was silent.

ᔕᔕᔕᔕ

Eurymachus sent a messenger to the men who waited to ambush Telemachus. "Come back," he told them. "Our plans have changed, thanks to

Penelope." All the suitors came back quickly to the palace.

Helen sniffed with her sharp nose. "Penelope's a sly one," she said. "I see her plan. You'll all give her magnificent gifts. Everybody will want to give a better present than anybody else. She complains that you've been making her poor, eating and drinking here for all these years. It looks to me as if you're going to make her rich again, richer than she's ever been."

"So much the better for me, when I marry her." Eurymachus was delighted. He sent his servants to fetch his gifts, but many of the suitors didn't trust their servants or weren't sure what treasures they would give. Some of the men lived on Ithaca, but many came from other islands, and some came from the mainland. They all moved as quickly as they could. As days and then weeks went by, they straggled back, loaded with gifts. Penelope would not accept anything, however, until everybody was ready.

Some suitors brought gifts of animals: sheep, cattle, pigs. Special pens had to be built. The animals had to be fed and watered. The pens had to be mucked out. The servants were on their feet from dawn to dark. Often their masters had to put on old clothes and pitch in themselves. Other suitors brought carved thrones, bronze tripods, silver basins and golden pitchers, leather sacks of grain and huge jars of ruby wine and sweet-smelling oil. Where could the precious things be kept? Who would guard them? Tempers flared. Rarely a day went by without a fight. Kleea threw up her hands in disgust. "The gods themselves couldn't keep order here," she said.

Many suitors had not returned when Penelope's weaving was finished and the cloth at last taken down from the great loom. Kleea and Aleta and other women unrolled it. They gazed in wonder. "Oh!" gasped Aleta. The border was ivy leaves of gold and silver. Scenes from the king's life seemed about to jump off the fabric: a boar hunt, a chariot battle, a feast at the palace, a grape harvest at the farm. Young Odysseus, holding his bow, bent his head to receive the victor's wreath from his father's hand. Nobody had ever seen such work. "It's a marvel," they declared. "Athene must have been standing by the weaver's side." Penelope agreed. She knew it was much the best work she had ever done. The women folded the precious thing and carried it to the great storeroom. Penelope chose a carved chest, inlaid with designs in gold and ivory, and Kleea locked the shroud away to await old King Laertes' death.

"Let's hope it stays here for many years," she said.

Finally the last suitor returned. "You took long enough," the others grumbled. "Did you go all the way to Egypt?" Now they spent their days presenting their rich gifts to the queen and showing off to each other.

Castor gave her a pair of proud horses, matched blacks, along with a slave to look after them. "Very fine indeed," Penelope admitted, "although Ithaca is a poor place for horses, all cliffs and crags. This would be a splendid gift for a young man on the mainland. Perhaps Telemachus will want to move." She smiled.

Antinous brought many gifts, but Penelope lingered a long time over a brooch made of pure gold. On the brooch, a golden hunting dog held down a golden fawn and ripped its throat. "Are you offended?" Antinous asked at last. "It's not the most suitable scene for a lady."

"A great artist did this work," Penelope replied. "Hephaestus himself could be proud of it. Kleea, look at this," she said.

Kleea took the brooch. "Oh!" She let out her breath in a long sigh.

"Yes." Penelope's voice was somewhere between laughter and tears. "My father gave Odysseus a brooch like this, though not so large. He pinned his cloak back with it when he left for Troy." Her eyes misted over. Quietly, Antinous put his next gift in front of her. It was a mirror of polished bronze, with an ebony handle. Penelope looked at her reflection and

burst out laughing. "I'm getting old," she declared. "Why on earth do you want to marry me?"

Poor Antinous! "I can't please you, can I," he said sadly.

Penelope was touched, but only for a moment. "Aleta, keep this mirror for me." She handed it to the girl. "You have more use for it than I do."

The procession of gifts went on. Kleea and Aleta made a display of precious things. Jars of wine and oil and sacks of grain were marked with the giver's seal. Animals were put in the care of the proper herdsmen.

The cowherd and his son drove the fat cattle to pasture. "We'll need extra hay to get them through the winter," the cowherd told Penelope. "It's a pity they didn't give feed along with the gift."

The shepherd and his dogs took the new flock of sheep up to the hills. "We can look after all of them," he said.

"The sooner these pigs get into the acorns, the better," said the swineherd. "I'll send for the lads to drive them home."

The days passed quickly, but the nights were long and slow. At night, Penelope turned her thoughts toward her son. Was he safe? Would he be home before the contest? Why had she fixed the date for it so soon?

She could not know it, but Telemachus was safe. His ship had been blown out of its usual course, and he had landed almost a day's journey away, near a high cliff. "I know this cliff," he told his crew. "Giant oak trees grow below it. Acorns cover the ground. We keep our pigs here. See, that's the smoke from the swineherd's hearth. Stay with the ship, men, while I go and see him."

"Have the gods sent you?" asked the swineherd. "You're just the man I needed to see. Come and meet a guest who was thrown up on our shores. He knew your father years ago. Poor fellow, he has nothing but the rags on his back. He needs a place to live, food and clothes, and a warm fire now that winter's coming. I told him I was sure you'd help. Wasn't I right?"

"Absolutely," agreed Telemachus. He smiled at the old stranger, who warmed his hands at the fire. "A friend of my father's, were you? I want to hear all about it. It won't be easy to help you, though, with that gang in the palace watching everything I do." He shook his head. "It's time I got home. Who knows what those men have been up to all these months? I'm worried about my mother." Now he nodded briskly. "We won't arrive together," he decided. "Let's not let them know we've met before. I'll leave at sunrise tomorrow. You two must wait until mid-morning. Come along together when you bring the pigs to be slaughtered for the suitors' dinner."

When Telemachus entered the palace the next day, Eurymachus was the first to notice him. "Don't think you're going to be king," Eurymachus taunted. "Your mother took her time, but she's finally decided to marry one of us. The man she chooses will rule in Ithaca."

"The man she chooses will be king," Telemachus agreed. "When that happens. Excuse me, Eurymachus," he added politely, "I must let Mother know I'm home."

Aleta raced ahead of him. She knocked joyfully at the queen's door, but did not wait for an answer. Penelope and Kleea read the good news in her shining face. Telemachus came almost on her heels. The air was electric with messages, handclasps, hugs. Everybody talked and everybody listened. At last the room began to get calm.

"Aleta," asked Telemachus, "do something for me, please. Go outside and watch for the swineherd. There's an old beggar with him. He knew my father – I'll tell you all about it, Mother – and I've promised to help him. I don't want him to get off to a bad start in this house. Make him welcome, will you, he's a good old soul."

Aleta picked up her cloak. She passed Nesta in the great hall. Since her day at the shrine, Aleta no longer tried to speak to her mother. She avoided her mother's eyes. Nesta watched as Aleta paused in the doorway to put on her cloak before she went out.

Compost and garbage were piled up by the gate. Although it was cold outside, the pile was still working, generating some heat. An old dog had dragged himself onto the pile, or had been thrown there to die. Helen came out. She's watching me, thought Aleta. She's angry at me. These days, she's always angry.

Helen walked briskly toward the wool shed. As she went by the compost pile, she aimed a vicious kick. The dog jerked a little and tried to get up, but without success. The swineherd and the old beggar came through the gate just in time to see Helen's kick and watch her vanish into the shed. "The suitors won't treat you much better," remarked the swineherd, "you'd better be prepared."

"I've been badly treated before," said the beggar, "but I'm not as helpless as that dog."

The old dog pricked up his ears. The beggar looked. He looked again, and a tear came into his eye. He brushed it away. "Poor old creature," he said, "he's not good for much. Old age happens to all of us, though, unless we die young. He's got good lines, hasn't he, might have been a fine hunter once."

"The best," agreed the swineherd. "He was trained by the great Odysseus, though his master sailed away to fight at Troy when that dog was still a puppy. The huntsmen could send him after the fastest game: wild goats, rabbits, even deer. He followed a scent better than any dog I ever knew. Argus, that's his name."

"Argus," said the beggar slowly. The dog could not get up, but now his ears went down and his tail thumped weakly on the ground.

"It's shameful, how he's treated," added the swineherd. "A dog gets in a bad way when his master is gone. Servants don't look after him." He walked on and entered the great house. As for old Argus, he had heard again a voice he had longed to hear, and he was content. He closed his eyes and died.

CHAPTER NINE

NEWS
FOR PENELOPE

A leta brought wine and water for the visitors, then she ran upstairs. She found Telemachus in his mother's hall in the women's quarters. The great loom had been moved back where it belonged, on the far side of the tables where the queen and her maids were sitting at their meal. A new piece of weaving glowed rich dark red against the white plastered wall.

Everybody watched Aleta as she slid into her seat beside her grandmother. Helen was nearby, Nesta not far away. "You know that beggar Telemachus was telling us about? He's downstairs now," Aleta told them. "The swineherd's with him. He's a ragged old man with a bald head, and he stinks, but bad luck can happen to anybody. I got bread for him and a plate of meat and some wine, but the men have been giving him a bad time."

"It's disgusting, that a guest is insulted in this house," exclaimed Kleea, "and we can't do a thing about it."

"We've had time to get used to it," said Penelope. "I get angry, but not as angry as I used to. Is the old man doing anything to provoke them?"

"At first he sat by the door and kept out of the way," answered Aleta, "but then he started going around and asking all of them for some scraps from their plate. Most of them gave him a little bit, but not Antinous. He hit the old man on the shoulder with a stool."

"Antinous hit him?" exclaimed Penelope. "I thought better of Antinous."

"Shame," cried Kleea.

"That's what the others said. The old man said he hoped Antinous would be dead before his wedding day. There would have been a fight, I'm sure, Antinous was getting up, but the others shamed him. 'That's no way to treat a beggar,' they said. 'What if he turns out to be a god in disguise? That could happen, and you'd be as good as dead.' Now the old man is sitting by the door again, trying to stay out of the way. He's a nice old man, even if he does stink, and he thanked me like a gentleman. I hope they leave him alone."

"I'll go down." Telemachus stood up.

"Bring the swineherd to me," Penelope told him.

She spoke quietly to the swineherd. "Ask the stranger to come here. From what I hear, he'll be safer upstairs than down. Has he been to far places? I'd like to ask him about my husband. Do you think I should?"

"My Queen," replied the swineherd, "I could listen to the man's stories all night and all day too. He says he knew Odysseus long ago. Lady, he has wonderful news, if it's true. I didn't say anything about it to Telemachus in case it's just another rumour, but this stranger has heard that the king your husband is alive and well. Perhaps he will soon be home."

"If only I could believe it!" Penelope leaned forward. "I must talk to him myself. Men have come before, pretending to be messengers from

Odysseus, telling me stories about him, but they were all liars."

"Another woman could have been fooled."

"I was fooled a time or two, years ago. I learned to be suspicious. I learned to set my traps. After a while, the liars gave up. I'll give this old man a rich tunic and a warm cloak if he can really give me news. With the gods' help, Odysseus and Telemachus would soon get rid of the gang downstairs. Do you think the gods would help us?"

"Zeus could hit a few of them lazy dimwits with his thunderbolts, it wouldn't surprise me." The swineherd smiled gleefully. "Wouldn't I like to see it!"

As he spoke, Telemachus, downstairs, gave a huge sneeze that echoed through the house. Penelope laughed. "Did you hear that sneeze? That's an omen that everything we just said is going to come true. Death to the suitors, every one! Go and get the stranger."

"I'll be glad to bring her all my news," the stranger promised, "but later, when it's dark and those thugs won't notice me. They threw a stool already, and they've drunk more wine since then. Somebody might decide to skewer me on his sword."

"That man is no fool," agreed Penelope, "we'll have more privacy after the sun goes down."

Helen nodded to Nesta and some of the other women. "It's time we went downstairs to help serve dinner," she said.

"Time to join the party, you mean," snapped Kleea.

Nesta blushed, Helen laughed. Helen didn't care a rap for Kleea, but she badly wanted to see what was happening downstairs. Eurymachus was slipping away from her, she could feel it. Helen had always been angry; now she was frightened as well. Fear was a new feeling. She hated it, and she didn't understand it, and this made her more angry still. Without Eurymachus, how could she ever get away? Helen was curious about the beggar. Where had he come from? Who might he be? Could she find out something about him that Eurymachus might be glad to know?

A few minutes later, Aleta followed Helen and Nesta down the stairs. "Help the others with dinner," Kleea had told her. "See what's happening and bring us word." Aleta wished she had not belittled the beggar. Even though he was ragged and smelly, he was a person to be reckoned with, she was sure of that. She ran down eagerly.

In the middle of the great hall, tables and benches had been pulled back to make a space. The scruffy stranger faced another ragged tramp, both with fists raised. Eurymachus gave the signal, and the beggar's fist connected with the other's jaw. Down he went, spitting teeth. Castor almost doubled up with laughter. "We offered him a pudding for his prize," the big man chuckled. "Get one, Nesta, and take it to him." He gave her a push.

The beggar put the pudding in his ragged knapsack. His face was red and his jaw set. Nesta shrank back. This man might be a beggar now, but he had not always been poor and powerless. The old man pushed her away a little with his foot.

Helen watched from the shelter of one of the great pillars. She made her way back to Eurymachus. "There's something about that beggar," she said grimly. "He's a warrior, isn't he."

"Has been, likely," Eurymachus nodded, "but that fight doesn't mean a thing. The other fellow is nothing but an oversized sack of guts. He tried to run away as soon as the old man took off his tunic. I wish I had biceps like that myself! We made the coward stay and fight. It's the best laugh I've had in years! We're keeping the old man as our official beggar."

Helen smiled. "I'll try to stay near the queen," she said. "She's sent for that beggar. I'll pick up what I can."

ﬗﬗﬗﬗ

Penelope worked at her loom for a short time, but she couldn't settle to her weaving. Soon she threw down the shuttle. "I'm restless," she said. "Help me dress, Aleta, and fetch your grandmother to do my hair. I don't know why I should dress up for a beggar, but I'm going to, he's my son's guest and he's been insulted here. That's enough reason to honour him. Set rich chairs for both of us."

By the time the beggar was announced, Helen was leaning against the wall not far from Penelope. She had brought her spindle, and was industriously spinning hunks of wool into yarn for the queen to weave. Nesta, on a stool beside her, fed the wool into Helen's busy hands. In the big room, other women worked and chatted.

The queen sat straight in her inlaid chair. Silver, gold and polished stone shimmered in her dark hair. "Welcome, stranger," she greeted the old man. "Telemachus and I are both shamed by the way you've been treated. It pains me that I can't keep such things from happening. It seems that the gods have deserted my house."

The beggar nodded. He knew he should say something, but he could not speak. His eyes were stinging with tears. Penelope saw he was struggling, though she did not know why. She thought he was overcome with shyness, a beggar in the presence of a great lady like herself. How could she help him?

She pointed to a carved chair set near her own. "Sit down, stranger," she invited. "Make yourself comfortable. You walked a long way before you got here, didn't you. Let me send for a servant to wash your feet."

Helen stopped twirling her spindle. She put down her work and stepped briskly forward. Aleta had risen from her stool beside the queen. The beggar looked from one to the other. "Is there an old woman who might do this?" he asked. His voice cracked. "Somebody who wouldn't make fun of my spindly legs and wrinkled skin?"

"Of course," agreed Penelope. "Aleta, fetch your grandmother. You can carry the water and the basin for her."

Aleta darted off, returning almost at once. In one hand she held a golden pitcher, in the other a silver basin. She put them down and offered her hands to help Kleea kneel. "My bones are stiff," muttered the old woman. "I don't move fast any more."

"Take your time, mistress." The beggar had better control of himself now. Aleta set the silver basin in front of him. She undid his sandals and laid them aside. "Ah," he sighed, "that's just what I needed."

Kleea poured warm water from the golden pitcher. She took one calloused foot in her hands and massaged it gently. Then she lifted the pitcher again in her left hand and put his tunic out of the way, ready to begin to wash and massage his lower leg. The old man stiffened and twisted away.

Too late. The pitcher dropped from Kleea's hand, clattering on the floor. Water splashed everywhere. Her head jerked up, her faded eyes darkening with the shock of recognition. Her lips were already forming the word "Master!" when his strong hand closed round her throat, cutting off her breath. He hissed in her ear, "Kleea, not a word, as you value your life."

Kleea could not speak, could not move her head, but Odysseus, home at last, thought she had heard him. Would she, could she obey? Slowly, he loosened his hand.

Penelope had been watching Helen. The clatter of the pitcher startled her, and she spoke sharply, "Kleea, what's the matter with you? Hasn't our guest had enough trouble today? Bring more water, Aleta, and mind what you're doing."

Kleea bent her head. Her tears dropped on the leg she was massaging, but she kept her face hidden. Again and again her hands felt their way over the long scar on her master's leg. How well she knew it! She had bandaged that leg often enough before the wound was healed. Then, day after day, she had massaged it. She knew every ridge of that jagged scar.

Penelope could feel the tension. It was centred on him, the man leaning

forward over Kleea's bent grey head. Penelope wanted to take the stranger into her inner room where no one could see or hear them, but she knew she must not do that. She had never allowed one of the suitors into that room, even with other people present. Now, more than ever, she must not give her women an opportunity to gossip, to say "The queen was alone for hours with that old man."

"Draw your chair closer," she invited him. Kleea, still on her knees, pulled the silver basin out of the way. "What is your name, good stranger? Tell me about yourself. Tell me about your travels. I hear you have news of my husband, the lord Odysseus. I long to hear of him." How could she warn him to watch his words, here among her own women? The stranger swallowed and opened his mouth, but no words emerged.

"I've waited all these years," Penelope confided, leaning forward, "but now I don't think Odysseus will ever come back. A hundred suitors eat and drink here every day. They tell me it's time I got married again and they won't go away until I do. Some of my women agree with them." Her face was turned toward the stranger, away from Helen. She widened her eyes, trying to send a signal to him. He nodded just the least bit, but Penelope was sure he understood. She relaxed a little. Now she looked more carefully at the stranger. "It's odd," she said, "but I'm sure we've met. Perhaps you came here to Ithaca many years ago."

Helen took a deep breath. Why had Kleea dropped the pitcher? Was it no more than an old woman's stiff and clumsy hands?

The stranger's face gave nothing away. He shivered a little. Did Penelope know him, in spite of his beggar's disguise, in spite of not seeing him for almost twenty years? "No, lady," he lied smoothly. "I come from the south. I was born on the island of Crete. You wouldn't think it, to see me now, but I was a lord's son. I grew up in a great house." He laughed. "Fortunes change," he said lightly, "and mine has changed for the worse." He shrugged his shoulders.

Helen felt for her spindle and picked it up without taking her eyes off the scene. She turned her head this way and that, examining the old man. Was he really a native of Crete? Helen thought not. Her mother's mother had come all the way from Egypt, but she had lived in Crete. Helen knew how the Cretans talked.

"I admired Odysseus," the traveller continued. "He visited me on his way to Troy. That's when I first met him."

"You knew my husband!"

"It was long ago. He hoped to join forces with my brother. He was too late, they just missed each other. It wasn't his fault. Boreas, the North Wind, blew and blew. Odysseus could not get out of harbour for ten days. He stayed with me. I was rich at that time and looked after him well. He told me I would always be welcome in his home." Odysseus almost laughed aloud. It was fun to talk about himself this way. "What a man he was! A great warrior, of course, but other men fought well. That's not what made him special. No, Odysseus was famous for his trickery. They say he's the greatest trickster that ever lived, and I believe it. We Greeks would never have got inside the walls of Troy without him. We were ready to give up and sail away."

Odysseus was well launched into his story, happily telling his dear wife how clever he had been. Just in time, he realized he must not say one word about his adventures on the nine years' journey home. He could not tell Penelope how he was brought at last to Ithaca in an enchanted sleep, or how he was carried ashore wrapped in a roll of carpet and left sleeping on the beach. He could not tell her how Athene had come to disguise him, wrinkling his skin and stripping his head bare. Why, even his own wife was convinced that he was a poor old beggar, nothing more. Perhaps she would not recognize him later, when the time was right. What then?

"I'm certain that Odysseus is still alive," he said emphatically. "I heard of him last winter and thought he'd be here by now. I was looking forward to a place of honour, new clothing, a warm bed. My luck hasn't changed yet, the gods are still unkind." His voice was rueful.

"I rule for Odysseus here," replied Penelope. "I should be welcoming you the way he would. I won't offer you a place of honour, though. Somebody else might throw a stool at you. Or worse."

Penelope did not know whether to laugh or cry. This stranger had known Odysseus. Little bits of detail leaped into her heart: how he stood or sat, what weapons he used, his special kind of trickery – men were calling him the wily Odysseus long before he sailed away to Troy – even his skill as a builder. She could easily imagine his wooden horse, big enough to hide fifteen men in its belly. She could see the Trojans, poor fools, tearing down their walls to get the horse and its bellyful of Greek warriors inside the city.

Aleta, on her stool beside the queen, shivered with excitement. "You must put the suitors off again," she cried. "The king is coming home. You can't get married again now!"

Penelope was silent. "I have announced the contest," she said quietly. "I've said I'd marry the winner."

"There was some talk of this in the hall." Odysseus was thoughtful. "Now I understand. You have put this off for a long time, lady. It's difficult to postpone it any longer, even though your husband may not be far away."

"That's not the only problem," said Penelope quietly. "If he comes here, what value do you place on his life? A hundred men against one! If he reached the door, he wouldn't get more than one foot inside."

Helen did not move, but energy radiated from her. Where could he be, Odysseus? He couldn't be near home or they'd have heard something. Surely. But maybe not. The man was famous for his trickery. If he wasn't so old, I'd be wondering about this man right here, she thought. It can't be, though. Would the great Odysseus wear these stinking rags? Would the king let Antinous hit him with a stool? Would the queen fail to recognize him? No, no, impossible. But maybe not impossible. Best to tell Eurymachus.

Helen moved abruptly, knocking over her basket of wool. The queen's head and the beggar's turned in unison toward her. "Sorry," she murmured, and sank back again. She could not say anything to Eurymachus until she was certain, one way or the other. She could not afford to be wrong.

Aleta's mind too was busy. Unlike Helen, Aleta had seen Kleea's face when she dropped the pitcher of water. She had glimpsed the scar, had seen how her grandmother's hands caressed it, had felt the old woman's tears. All the time the stranger had been telling his stories, her grandmother had been sitting quietly with her head scarf over her face. For all anybody knew, she was asleep, but Aleta did not think so. She was certain that her grandmother was listening avidly to every word.

Suddenly everything was clear. Aleta knew how Odysseus got that scar. The story was one of her grandmother's favourites. Young Odysseus was visiting his mother's family. While he was hunting with his uncles, a wild boar charged. The untried hunter met the attack with his lance, but slipped and fell on the muddy ground. The boar tore the youth's leg with its tusk. Odysseus looked into its wicked red eyes and felt its foul breath on his face. He knew he was going to die. Then the beast dropped dead beside him; the lance had pierced its heart. "Well done," said his grandfather. "That leg should heal, though you'll be limping for a long time, maybe for the rest of your life. Stay here until the wound has closed. Then we'll send you home with lots of gifts." Kleea recognized Odysseus because of the scar.

Why didn't Penelope recognize him? Surely she would know her own husband! Yes, thought Aleta, I think she knows him. Maybe she's not sure yet, but almost sure. I know why she doesn't say anything: Helen mustn't guess. Aleta forced herself not even to look in Helen's direction. Often Helen would know a person's thoughts, even though no words were spoken. It's a gift some people have. I wish I didn't know this secret, Aleta thought, aware suddenly that she had been sitting still for hours, that her left leg was cramped, and that she needed to use the chamber pot. The feeling of urgency was not confined to her bladder. For good or evil, the long time of waiting was almost over.

The queen was talking about the contest she had planned. "There's a feat Odysseus used to perform with bow and arrows," she said, "but I've never seen anybody else manage it. We'll set up twelve double axes in one straight row in the hall, the way he used to do. Odysseus's great bow still hangs where he left it. Every man in turn will have his chance to bend that bow and string it, then to shoot an arrow through the axes. That's my test. Perhaps nobody will succeed. Then I'll have a little extra time." She frowned. "Everything is moving so quickly."

Odysseus rose to his feet. "They'll talk about this contest for a long time," he said. "Tomorrow is as good a day as another, it seems to me. You've done the best you can. Let the gods decide the outcome. Odysseus will be proud of you, if he ever gets to know. Good night, lady. Thank you for your kindness to an old beggar."

"An old beggar who helped my husband," said Penelope sharply. "You shall have the new cloak Odysseus would have given you, and a good tunic too. Kleea, Helen, make up a bed for this old man upstairs here, outside my room."

"Pardon, lady," Odysseus replied, "I haven't slept in a real bed for so many years, I'd toss and turn all night. Let me sleep as I'm used to, on the floor in the hall. The cloak would be welcome, though. The safest place for me is the coldest place in the room, beside the outer door."

Penelope flushed angrily. "I have to admit it's better for you to sleep there," she agreed. "Nobody can complain that you're getting special treat-

132

ment. I hate your old bones to get stiff on the cold floor just because of those suitors. Aleta, find a warm cloak for our guest. See him settled downstairs, then come back to me. Tuck a cloak around your grandmother before you go, I'm sure she's fallen asleep. Helen, let me see that yarn."

Helen had made her bow and had started toward the stairs. Now she turned back, her golden eyes glowing as Odysseus shambled past. The queen might delay her, but not for long. Whatever his secret, she would find it out!

Aleta followed Odysseus downstairs, a thick purple cloak in her arms. The key to the king's storeroom lay securely in the little pouch at her waist where her grandmother had put it only a moment before. Had Helen seen anything? Why had she stared at Odysseus so fiercely? The king has broad shoulders, Aleta thought, he's a match for Helen. She felt nervous but no longer terrified. Her grandmother had given her the king's key, and she would pass it on.

CHAPTER TEN

THE CONTEST
IS WON

O dysseus walked quietly toward the space by the door where he intended to sleep. As he passed the corridor leading to the great storeroom, Telemachus stepped forward and put a hand on his arm. "Come with me," he whispered. "Nobody will overhear us. We can talk in peace." Odysseus turned to follow the young man. Aleta took a torch and padded after them. It was like a dream. How could her grandmother know this was going to happen? Had Athene sent her a vision? Telemachus swung round toward the dim light. Aleta held out the key.

Without a word, Telemachus unlocked the door of the storeroom. Key in hand, he stood aside for the older man to enter, then beckoned Aleta to follow them. He looked at the key for a moment, then shrugged and handed it back to the girl. Shivering with excitement,

she watched him bolt the door, this time on the inside. He put his arm on the beggar's shoulder. "What can I do to make up for the way you've been treated?" he asked. "Your first day here, and you've been beaten already! I invited you. I'm ashamed."

Odysseus smiled a little. Telemachus was going to have a surprise! But Odysseus could not speak with the girl standing there. He looked at Aleta in irritation. "Take that cloak back to the hall," he ordered. "Wait for me by the door."

"Yes, Master." Aleta barely breathed the words, but Telemachus heard them.

"What's that?" he exclaimed.

When Aleta spoke, Odysseus moved in front of the heavy door. He smiled at Telemachus. His shoulders straightened at Athene's invisible touch. His wrinkled face became full again, his cheeks grew round, his eyes bright. "Goddess, I thank you once again," he murmured. "Soon you shall have a fitting sacrifice." He turned to Telemachus. "You were just a baby when I went away," he said softly, "but never a day has gone by, all these years, that I haven't thought of you. You've grown up well, my son. Taller than your father!" Odysseus chuckled.

Telemachus was totally still, as if some god had turned him to stone. His eyes grew very wide. He didn't blink. It was as if he couldn't bear to shut his eyes for even the tiniest part of a second. At last he gave a little cry and fell forward into his father's waiting arms.

Finally the two men held each other apart, at arm's length, though they did not let go. Both faces were wet. Tears coursed down Aleta's cheeks as well. Odysseus looked at her. "This is bad," he said. "Kleea recognized me, that's unlucky, but she'll be quiet. But this child? Why did you call me Master? How did you know?"

"I saw your scar," said Aleta bravely. "My grandmother has often told me how you got it. I saw her face. I knew it must be you."

"Very unlucky," exclaimed Odysseus. "Who else was watching? That woman with her spindle?"

"Helen," whispered Aleta.

"Dangerous," said Telemachus. "Aleta, is there any chance she guessed?"

"Who can tell?" Aleta fretted. "I couldn't see anything in her face, but I dared not look too close. I couldn't stare at her."

"That's no good." Odysseus was frustrated. "This is no time to take chances. Telemachus, we ought to kill both of them."

"What!" Telemachus stared at his father, then his shocked eyes turned to Aleta. His arm reached out to draw the shivering youngster to his side. "Aleta is Kleea's granddaughter, Father. We keep our birthdays together."

Aleta drew a deep breath. She looked up at Odysseus. Their eyes locked. "Well?" he demanded.

Well, what? What was he asking her? She was shaking again. Once, twice she tried to speak. "I would die," she got the words out at last. "For the queen."

Odysseus laughed grimly. "Die, would you?" he asked. "Have you ever seen anybody die?" Aleta shook her head. "I thought not. Don't talk lightly about it, girl. You're brave enough, I can see that. Are you clever too? Your grandmother gave away this secret, to you. What do you think, Telemachus, can this child manage not to give it away to anybody else?"

"Aleta knows her grandmother very well, or she would never have guessed," replied Telemachus, still holding her tight. "Kleea has been keeping secrets since before I was born. Aleta takes after her grandmother. She's young, and Kleea's old. All the same, there's nobody I'd trust more than the two of them. We have many enemies here, Father; we need all our friends."

"True enough," agreed Odysseus. "Aleta, I'm letting you live. Don't ever make me feel I made a mistake." Aleta gulped, but no words came out. She nodded and nodded again. Odysseus locked eyes with Telemachus.

"This Helen, now, what about her?"

"That's a different story," Telemachus told him. "She's in league with the suitors. She was watching you and Kleea. How do we know what she might have guessed? I don't think killing her is a good idea, though. She might have said something to one of the suitors, or to Aleta's mother."

"Then we'll get her out of the way until we can find out," Odysseus decided. "How can we do it?" He looked at Telemachus and then down at Aleta.

The girl took a deep breath. "I could tell Helen that my mother wants her," she suggested.

"Perfect, as long as your mother isn't in sight." Suddenly aware of how tight he had been holding his young friend, Telemachus released his grip. "Bring Helen to us. I'll wait until she comes through that door. Father, do you agree?"

Odysseus nodded. Why would Helen come to Aleta's mother? He didn't know, but that seemed unimportant. No doubt Telemachus would explain.

Aleta's bare feet dragged along the corridor. Maybe Helen would be sitting beside Eurymachus, whispering to him. Maybe she would be wrapped in his cloak. Maybe Aleta wouldn't find her at all. If she did, why would Helen listen to her? Even if she listened, why would she believe?

Most often a thing is harder than you expect, but sometimes it is easier. Aleta didn't have to look for Helen; Helen was waiting. Aleta hadn't taken two quiet steps into the hall when Helen pounced. Aleta struggled and kicked before she saw the dark face and gleaming eyes. Helen got a wiry hand on Aleta's throat. "I saw you creep into that passage. Now I've got you," she hissed, "and I'll have some answers. Not a sound, if you want to keep on living." She half-pushed, half-carried Aleta back into the dark corridor. The place

was full of little rustling sounds, mice possibly, nothing human. Helen's arms were cruelly strong. As Aleta's eyes adjusted again to the darkness, she was able to see the outline of the storeroom door. "Now we'll talk. What were you doing here? I know you've got the key." Helen's whisper was louder now. "I saw Kleea give it to you, don't think I didn't. Give it to me." A relentless hand moved from Aleta's throat down to the bag at her waist.

"I'll give it to you," whispered Aleta, thanking whatever god had guided Telemachus to give her back the key. She hadn't locked the door behind her, though. Of course she hadn't locked the door. How could she keep Helen from finding out that two men were hiding behind it? The cruel hands relaxed a little, and Aleta took out the great key. Helen grabbed it and pushed it in. She turned the key and shoved at the door. It did not budge.

"Hera guide me," said Helen in disgust. "What's wrong with this lock?" Again she turned the key. Now the door swung inwards. With one arm still locked around Aleta, Helen pushed forward.

The next few minutes were a blur of bodies. Telemachus and Odysseus had the advantage of surprise, but Helen was amazingly strong. Her neck and shoulders were slippery with sweet-smelling oil, which she managed to spread onto her arms and hands. She was like a fish, impossible to hold. Aleta, in her dark clothes, was bounced and jounced in the struggle. If Helen too had been wearing a dark tunic, she might have escaped, but her garment was a light cream colour, her favourite, and it betrayed her. Aleta grabbed two handfuls of it and hung on.

Then Helen was face down on the floor with Telemachus sitting on her. He got hold of one of her slippery arms and wiped it on his cloak. Then the other. All four people gulped for air. Aleta could hear her heart thudding. Odysseus untied the rope holding his rags together at the waist and knelt to tie Helen's hands behind her. With the strap from one of his

sandals, he bound her legs and ankles. Telemachus rolled her over.

"Did she talk to anyone out there?" hissed Odysseus.

"I don't know," gulped Aleta. With a corner of her skirt, she dabbed at her tears.

"I talked." Helen's voice dripped venom. "I told Eurymachus you were here, Odysseus, Sacker of Cities. He'll be ready for you."

"Come here with me." Telemachus led Aleta behind one of the chariot bodies on the other side of the room. "Sit down, little friend. Let's get our breath and think a little. We both know Helen pretty well, don't we, you even better than me. She could be telling the truth, but I think she's lying. I've tried to wake Eurymachus a time or two when he's snoring. It's not easy, and she didn't have much time. Was he with her in the hall?"

Aleta smiled at Telemachus. Already she felt easier. "I don't think so," she told him. "I'm pretty sure he wasn't. It all happened fast, but I didn't see anything. I didn't hear anything. She wanted to ask me questions." Suddenly Aleta heard a whisper of sound. She looked up. Odysseus was smiling down at her. She could see his white teeth and, dimly, his dark face.

"So, she was guessing who I might be. I thought as much. We'll gag her for now," Odysseus decided. He was already taking the strap from his other sandal and tearing a strip from his smelly rags. "You're a good friend, Aleta, Telemachus was right. Now get up to bed, child. Sleep well, Helen can't get away. My son and I have work to do."

Aleta slipped into the hall, but this time no hands grabbed at her. Nobody stirred, though more suitors than usual were sleeping against the wall. The air vibrated lightly with their snores. She tiptoed toward them. All the torches had burned out. Most of the heavy shutters had been closed against the wintry air, but one or two were partly open. Little patches of moonlight glimmered here and there. Could she see Eurymachus? His cloak was blue, trimmed with wolf fur. Was that it? Aleta couldn't see the sleeper's face, and the cloak looked different too, lighter where the moon caught it and darker in the shadows, but she could see his hair, light as straw, and the bald patch on top. Yes, Helen had been lying. Eurymachus was asleep and they were safe.

She ran back to tell the others and overtook Odysseus in the corridor, again disguised as the ragged old beggar. He staggered under a load of spears. "Good girl, that's a comfort." He leaned the spears against the wall. "We'll be busy in the storeroom tonight," he explained. "I want Helen locked up somewhere else. Upstairs, I think. Wake your grandmother, Aleta, and tell her. Telemachus will bring the woman up. Off with you now." He smiled and patted her shoulder.

Aleta slept well, and so did Odysseus and Telemachus, though not until much later. They had work to do in the room where the sleepers lay. In that great hall, banks of spears stood in their stands on either side of the outer door. Beside them on one side were bows and arrows. Swords and great axes lined the remainder of the other wall, along with shields of different shapes — the huge full-body shields of the past and the smaller round shields that had replaced them in battle.

On Odysseus's orders, Telemachus fetched the swineherd and the cowherd. Telemachus told them, "It's not safe to have these weapons within reach of our enemies. Antinous attacked this old beggar with a stool tonight. Another time, one of these idiots might pick up a spear, or a sword, or perhaps a bow and arrow. We could have a very ugly fight. I should have thought of this before. Help me put all these weapons into the storeroom. I'll feel safer when I've turned the key in the lock."

Once, a spear clattered to the floor. "Shhh," hissed Telemachus. They all froze. Here and there, a sleeper stirred. Nesta, curled up beside

Castor, opened a drowsy eye. She looked around without seeing what was happening, rolled over and slept again.

Upstairs, Helen did not sleep. Kleea had taken cloaks and blankets out of a big chest, and Telemachus had dumped her in. The heavy lid was held closed by a wooden peg through the hasp. Helen lay on the hard wood with bent knees, on her side, still tied and gagged. Luckily for her, the chest was old and the back board had split. She had air to breathe.

"Something has changed," said Eurymachus irritably the next morning. "Something is different. What is it?" He looked around, without seeing just what had changed. Helen was missing, and he kept looking for her. Along one long wall, all the shutters had been opened and fastened back inside. There was no wind and the winter sun was bright, but the room was cold. The suitors wrapped their cloaks close to their bodies.

Eurymachus didn't have much time to think. Telemachus called Kleea and the women to clear a wide path in the centre of the hall, from one end to the other. They moved the tables out of the way and set chairs and stools along the walls at each side. They lifted Penelope's carved chair and a few other seats onto a raised platform. From the storeroom they carried woven baskets, heavy with great double axeheads. The old beggar whispered a few words in Kleea's ear and then took his place at the far end of the hall beside the outer door. Aleta stared at the hole in the axeheads. What man could possibly shoot an arrow through these small openings? Could even a god shoot as well as that?

Telemachus stepped into the middle of the cleared space. "Here's where the axes are to stand," he announced. "My mother will choose her new husband today, if any man here can string my father's bow and shoot an arrow through all twelve of them." Two men held a long cord, one at each end of the hall. Other men dug a trench, using the string as a guide. Telemachus knelt at the far end and sighted along the trench. It looked straight, but he wished he could borrow Mentor's far-seeing eyes.

"Bring earth and pile it up, to hold the axes straight," he commanded. "The holes must line up exactly." The suitors ordered their servants to help carry the earth. They watched curiously as Telemachus positioned the double axeheads, measuring the distance between each of them, and the height of each hole above the floor. The job took most of the morning, but by noon everything was ready.

Penelope came down, attended by her maids. The queen wore her richest dress, a long tunic of deep purple wool. Gold threads, woven into the delicate cloth, shimmered in the winter sun. The queen stood like a goddess, beautiful and terrible. A hush fell on the hall.

"Today I will choose a husband," her voice rang out, echoing in the big room. "Today is midwinter, the shortest day, a good day for a hard choice. We have waited a long time, though I have waited longer than you have. The time of waiting is over. Telemachus, bring me your father's bow."

In the silence, Telemachus brought the great black bow and put it in his mother's hand. "Odysseus used to string this bow," the queen continued. "He could send an arrow whistling through the axes standing there. It's not easy. No doubt a god could make the shot, but I never saw another man succeed. Surely one of you will do it, though, and he must be the best among you. That's the man I will marry, a man as good as Odysseus. Take your turns, gentlemen."

The suitors looked at each other. Noise filled the hall, as they tried to decide who should begin. "The most important men should be first," suggested Castor. "Eurymachus, you should start."

Would Antinous agree? Eurymachus looked at him. "By all means," said Antinous pleasantly. "We'll all get our chance."

Eurymachus had won many prizes for his archery. He took the great bow proudly and set out to bend it so that he could slip the bowstring into its groove. Telemachus waited beside him with a quiver full of arrows. The bow bent a little, but not nearly enough. Eurymachus leaned on it. His face

grew red with effort. Muscles in his arms and back felt the strain. Again and again he tried. At last he threw the bow to the floor. "No man can bend this bow," he said. "Try it for yourselves." He looked angrily at the others.

"If nobody else succeeds, you can try again later," Castor soothed him. "Penelope, you've set up this contest, do you agree? We can go on trying until one of us succeeds, or until everybody gives up?"

"I'll decide that when the time comes," replied the queen. "Eurymachus has done his best. If no one succeeds, perhaps I should change the contest. But every man must have his chance."

One after another, the suitors took up the great bow and tried to bend it. Each man in turn tried every way he knew. As the day went on, one after another gave up the contest and went to sit sullenly and nurse his aching muscles. It was late afternoon before all the suitors had made their trial. Not a single arrow had been shot. Nobody could string the bow!

Eurymachus rose to his feet. "Lady," he raged, "you've made fools of us again. Now I will bend this bow. Or I'll take an axe to it and we'll change the contest."

"Wait a minute," Telemachus interrupted, "one man here has not yet had his turn." The old beggar came forward and held his hand out for the bow.

A great roar of laughter went up from the suitors. They were all feeling like idiots, and even a little thing would have given them an excuse to laugh, but he did look silly, the ragged, bald old man holding the great bow.

"Take it away from him," snorted Eurymachus. "It's an insult to your mother, Telemachus. He certainly won't be able to bend that bow, but if by some strange chance he was able to do it, would you expect your mother to marry him?"

Penelope rose to her feet. "Every man in this hall is to have his chance," she repeated, "this old man too. Are you afraid he will be able to do what you cannot?"

Eurymachus was afraid of exactly that, but he could hardly say so. He stood back. Antinous chuckled. "Let him make a fool of himself too," he said. "He looks a lot sillier than we did." Some of the others laughed.

The old man looked around. Telemachus stood by his side. The cowherd and the swineherd were behind him, one on each side of the great door. In one smooth action, he bent and strung the bow. As if they'd been a single person, the hundred suitors gasped. Aleta shivered with excitement. "Help him, Athene," she whispered under her breath. "Great goddess, guide his arm."

The beggar pulled a stool in front of the axes and sat down, holding the black bow. He bent his ear to the string and plucked it gently, listening to its sound. He lifted the bow and examined it slowly, carefully. He ran the calloused thumb and forefinger of his right hand down the string. At last he nodded and held his hand out for the arrow. Now all his movements were swift and sure. Easily, casually almost, he raised the bow. Without getting up from the stool, he sent the arrow whistling through the axeheads.

"Death," yelled Eurymachus, his voice rising above the shouting. He drew his sword and rushed toward the beggar.

"Death," replied Odysseus. He took a second arrow from Telemachus's waiting hand and sent it through his enemy's throat. Eurymachus fell, his bright blood staining the floor.

The suitors stood dazed, not yet taking in the fact that Eurymachus, their leader, was dead. Now Odysseus rose to his feet, bow in hand, a third arrow ready to let fly. He stood like a king, straight and proud. "Kleea, Aleta, take your mistress upstairs," he commanded. "All you women, follow the queen. Bolt the door after you. Don't come down until I summon you, no matter what you hear."

Penelope turned, a curious smile on her lips. Aleta held open the door while the queen passed through and the other women followed. The door closed. In the silent hall, the men heard the bolt slide home.

Upstairs, Penelope faced her women. Fierce joy swelled her heart. "I have found a champion," she said. "Surely a god bent that bow and aimed the arrow truly. Eurymachus is dead. He got what he deserved." She went into her room and closed the door.

Kleea called Aleta over to the chest. She pulled out the wooden pin. Together they lifted the heavy lid. Helen twisted her head to look up. Her tawny eyes were dull. The gag held her mouth open. Her face was slack, as if all her muscles had atrophied.

"Eurymachus is dead." Kleea said it brutally. Helen blinked, but her face did not change. "Help me get her out," said Kleea to Aleta. "No, get your mother to help. We'll keep her feet tied, but I think the fight's gone out of her. Death is looking for her, but he hasn't found her yet."

Nesta carried Helen over to a corner near the loom, and sat with her arms around her one-time friend. Helen's head lay against Nesta's shoulder. "Odysseus has come home," she said dully. "That old man, it was Odysseus all the time. He's back, and we'll all be killed."

"Not possible," Nesta protested.

"It's true, it's got to be, nothing else makes sense. He's home, and we're dead."

"Helen, don't talk like that. You've always been angry, you've always been brave."

"You didn't guess that I was terrified?"

"You, Helen, terrified?" Nesta shook her head.

"It's your turn now, Nesta. You've got a chance, with your mother and your daughter. Not me. It doesn't matter much." The dull voice gathered energy. "I wanted to run the household for Eurymachus."

"You're wrong about my chance," said Nesta. "Mother is harder on me than on any of the other women. She expects more from me. So much the worse for her. I hope you're wrong about that old beggar. If he is Odysseus, though, he's the one that doesn't have a chance, not us! Two

148

men, one too old to fight and one too young, and two farmers who haven't
ever been in battle, against a hundred men from our best families! Lift up
your face and look at me, Helen. That's no contest."

Helen lifted her face. She was not crying, though her eyes looked huge,
like molten gold in her pallid face. Kleea came over. "Nesta, help Helen
wash her face," she said. "Then come and put out food for all of us. We
must be ready."

Ready for what? Nobody knew. The air was full of ghastly sounds from
downstairs, screams muted by the thick wooden walls and floor. Often,
the tables and benches shook and shivered, as if an earthquake had struck,
followed by aftershocks, some small, some large. The seated women trembled with each shock, learning to brace their feet for balance and to chew
their bread carefully so as not to bite their tongues.

Safe in her inner room, Penelope stood at the window. Aleta had
opened the shutters and fastened them back against the wall. The queen
pulled her cloak around her and leaned out to look at the moon. "Do you
like to look at the night sky?" she asked.

"I love the moon and the stars." The queen moved a little to make room
for the girl to stand beside her. "I'm scared," Aleta confided.

"It's a time to be scared," Penelope agreed. "But look, the moon is
almost full. Artemis is gaining power. It's a hunter's moon. Artemis was a
huntress before she was goddess of the moon. That's a good omen, isn't it."

Slowly the long night wore on. The screams and thuds came less and
less often. At last the women couldn't hear anything. The hall was quiet. In
the silence, a fist pounded on the door. "Open up, Kleea. You know who's
speaking, it's me, Telemachus."

At her mother's nod, Nesta crept downstairs and slid back the bolt.
Telemachus walked slowly up the stairs, bringing with him the sweet,
sickly smell of blood. His tunic was no longer grey, it was almost all dark
red. Aleta held the inner door open for Penelope, who put her arms

around her son and held him close.

"It's over, Mother, they're dead." A shout of triumph rang through the room.

"All of them?" asked Penelope.

"All but two, the singer and the herald. They did not deserve to die."

"I'll go down," said Penelope.

"Please don't," replied Telemachus. "Not yet. Wait until the hall is clean. While you're waiting, you can get ready to welcome your husband." He grinned, and ruffled her hair.

Penelope stiffened. "Who, that old man? If you think he's Odysseus, you've been tricked. He won't fool me."

"We'll see," replied Telemachus. He patted his mother's shoulder. "You'll be able to make up your own mind. Nobody's going to do it for you." He paused. "I've come for some women, the disloyal ones. There's work for them downstairs."

Kleea rounded up the twelve women, some crying and others dry-eyed and shivering. Telemachus looked down at Helen. "Untie her legs," he commanded. "Get her up. There's work for her to do." Helen stood with difficulty. She leaned on Nesta as they walked over to the others. Suddenly Aleta rushed to her mother and hugged her. Nesta looked surprised, but she returned the hug. Aleta was crying. After a moment, Nesta pushed the girl roughly away.

"Move," Telemachus snapped, and the women disappeared down the stairs.

Kleea jerked away from the sight of Nesta's vanishing head. She could feel pain gathering in her chest. She fought for breath. With all her strength, she pushed the pain away. "This is a great day," she said at last.

"A day for rejoicing," Penelope agreed. Her shining eyes were fixed on the staircase, as if the hero was going to appear there right away. She straightened her shoulders. "The suitors would have killed Telemachus and

any of my people who got in their way, if fate had given them the chance."

Kleea tried to stop thinking about Nesta, or about her own ageing body. The pain had gone away, for the time. What could she do to help Penelope? "Aleta and I will get your bath ready," she said. "What are you going to wear? Your tunic with the gold threads? A little kohl around your eyes, and red ochre for your cheeks and lips. You want to look your best. Did you really believe it would happen? Odysseus, home after all these years!"

"Stop it, Kleea," Penelope cut in. "If Odysseus has really come back, he can see me without a painted face. If it is Odysseus. You may be certain, but I'm not. Hope has sprung in my heart too often. Now this stranger has fooled you and Telemachus as well. He must not fool me. I am very tired, though. I'll go and rest until the hall is cleaned."

CHAPTER ELEVEN

TREACHERY AND FAITHFULNESS HAVE THEIR REWARDS

I n the great hall, Odysseus looked at the women. They stood in a row facing him, heads lowered. "Drag the bodies outside. Look at the dead men while you're doing it, so you know what happens to traitors." The king's voice was harsh and cold. "Then scrub down the tables and benches and all the other furniture. Make sure you do it well." He turned away.

The two herdsmen scraped the floor with shovels while the women went about their grisly task. Tears streamed down some faces, while others were grey with shock. Telemachus stood nearby, a short sword in his hand.

"When this job is done, we're next," Helen said at last.

"Of course." Nesta's voice was dull and empty.

"Do you want to live?"

"Not much, what's the use? Do you?"

"I hate them." Helen was coming to life again. "Killing a hundred defenceless men, the butchers." She bent and rubbed her legs, where the strap had cut into them. Then she and Nesta went on dragging bodies outside, Nesta taking one leg and Helen the other.

"Four men against a hundred?" asked Nesta. "I'd say the hundred had their chance."

"We must get to their families. They'll take revenge. They'll kill the killers!"

"No, Helen." Nesta was firm at last. "This is enough blood." Each time they went out into the courtyard, the cold wind sliced at their sweating bodies. Against the wall, the pile of corpses grew larger. The cowherd guarded the outer gate.

"They're watching," said Helen. "We can't get out."

Again they turned back into the hall. The sweet stench of blood was still heavy in the air. Telemachus moved closer to the door. "Talk to him," muttered Helen.

"Lord Telemachus, what will you do with the bodies?" asked Nesta. "Can we give them decent burial?"

"They don't deserve it," replied Telemachus. "Are we to give them money for the ferryman? I don't think they would have done as much for us, if we had been lying there."

Nesta raised her eyes. She was thinking of Castor's spirit in the underworld. Without proper burial and money for the ferry, he would wander forever, unable to get across the swamp of Acheron.

"Telemachus," she pleaded. Then she saw Helen in the shadows behind Telemachus. Helen's arm was raised. In her hand glinted a small, wicked blade. Nesta was never a person who stopped to think. Now she jumped at Telemachus. He went down with her on top of him. Helen's knife plunged into Nesta's back.

Odysseus himself threw Helen and Nesta off his son. In lightning motion, he put a foot on Helen's chest and plunged his sharp sword into her throat. His eyes swung around the hall. Nobody moved. Telemachus sat up slowly, then got carefully to his feet. Father and son drew deep breaths.

"Nesta saved my life." Telemachus was surprised. Nesta lay on her side, knees curled up to her chest. Her eyes were closed, but the two men could hear her breathing, each breath a shuddering, noisy sucking in of pain. The knife handle stuck out under her left shoulder. "Should I draw it out?" Telemachus asked his father.

"No," replied Odysseus. "Lay her on one of the big shields. Carefully, now. Carry her upstairs to Kleea. If she can be helped, Kleea will help her. Hurry up, now, all of you. Let's be done with this."

While the people in the hall finished their grim task, Nesta lay curled on a narrow bed upstairs. Kleea sat beside her, breathing raggedly. "You may die now if I pull out the knife," Kleea told her, "but you'll surely die soon if I don't. What is your choice?"

Nesta said nothing. Again, Kleea felt the familiar pain. Could she push it back one more time? Why did Nesta look like that? Was she so sure her own mother would not even try to make her well? "You saved the life of Lord Telemachus," the old woman said at last. "I would use all my skill for my worst enemy, after that." She patted Nesta's shoulder awkwardly. Tears gathered in Nesta's eyes.

Kleea moved around behind the bed. Gently, she drew out the knife, pressing a folded woollen pad against the wound. Very soon, the white wool was sopping with dark blood. "I'll get bandages," said Kleea, "and a poultice to help stop the bleeding. Stay with your mother, Aleta. Change the pad and hold it tight."

Aleta held the pad with all her strength, smiling through her tears. Life held strange surprises. Aleta had longed to give her life for Penelope because of her mother's treachery. Now her mother had thrown herself in front of Helen's knife. Again and again she whispered, "Mother, please don't die" and "I'm proud of you, so proud."

At last Penelope appeared in the doorway of her room. Kleea rushed to her side. "I should have been helping you," she said, "but I couldn't. So much has been happening. And now your husband will be here any minute."

"Do I need help?" asked the queen. "While I slept, I dreamed that Athene touched me with her radiance. Was it a true dream?"

Kleea drew back and looked at her. "I've never seen you more beautiful," she replied at last. "Your skin is smooth and soft, your face is rosy and your eyes are bright. Threads of gold are wound into your dark hair. You're right, the goddess has been with you."

Now they heard the downstairs door swing open. Feet rang on the stairs. Telemachus came in first, with Odysseus right behind. The king too was changed. Athene had taken away the remains of his disguise. He was richly dressed. His blue eyes were sharp, his wrinkles had disappeared, and the chestnut curls had grown again on his head.

Penelope sat in her inlaid chair. On the other side of the room, Odysseus stood near the stairs. Nobody moved.

"Mother!" exclaimed Telemachus. "What kind of welcome is this for your husband?"

Penelope sat. Was this man really Odysseus, or was it another trick? Would she not know her husband? Would not her heart beat faster? She felt only a huge weariness. She did not want to look at the man. "Whoever you are," she admitted, "I'm grateful to you. I have ruled Ithaca as best I can for nearly twenty years. It's been more and more difficult lately, as you know. You have my deepest thanks."

Odysseus bowed slightly. Telemachus looked from one to the other. "This is ridiculous," he said, "the two of you across the room from each other, as if you'd never seen each other before."

"I'm tired," Penelope told them, "and you, whoever you are, must be exhausted. Maybe you are Odysseus and maybe not. We can talk more about it when both of us are rested."

"Mother, this is my father," cried Telemachus. "You're insulting him with these doubts."

"I don't mean to insult him," replied Penelope, "certainly not. I want to honour him. Kleea, Aleta, get some help to pull the great bed out of my room. Make it up the way you would for Odysseus, if he really was home after all these years. That's the master's bed, and this man shall sleep in it tonight."

Across the room, Odysseus laughed. "O my clever Penelope! I built that room and carved that bed myself when we were married. An old olive tree grew against the wall, and I built our room around the tree and used it to support the floor, leaving the trunk jutting through. Wife of mine, you know all this, even though nobody else knows it. Do you need me to remind you? I trimmed off the branches and cut the trunk to the size of a post and carved it to make one corner of our bed. That bed can't be moved, and well you know it. Unless —" He paused, and his face darkened. "Tell me at once, Penelope, has anybody dared to cut through that post?"

Penelope laughed joyously. Now at last she jumped to her feet and ran across the room with outstretched arms. Odysseus just had time to open his own arms before she was there and he was holding her warm to his heart. "Are you sure of me now, my wise Penelope?" he chuckled.

Penelope looked around the room and nodded. "Kleea, make sure that all our people are looked after," she said. "Odysseus and I have stories to tell each other and plans to make. Athene looks on us kindly. Perhaps that great goddess will hold back the dawn while we talk and sleep."